A FLIGHT
TO
NOWHERE

PEP CLUBB

Order this book online at www.trafford.com
or email orders@trafford.com

Most Trafford titles are also available at major online book retailers.

Printed in the United States of America.

ISBN: 978-1-4669-9930-5 (sc)
ISBN: 978-1-4669-9929-9 (e)

Trafford rev. 06/07/2013

www.trafford.com

North America & international
toll-free: 1 888 232 4444 (USA & Canada)
phone: 250 383 6864 ♦ fax: 812 355 4082

#1

Russell Willow, an ex-fighter pilot in the Korean war, had a charter service and took eight retired school teachers, to Barbados for a summer vacation when the fun was over, and had to leave, the weather service there told him that there was a storm coming there way, but that he should be in the State's and would out run the storm, in an hour and a half, then one hell of a storm caught up with them, Russ being a very good pilot, kept his plane in the air when it was about to run out of fuel. he discovered an uncharted Island with the Fountain of youth, and a food that looked like eggplant, growing on tree's, that tasted like what ever you wanted to eat, that some how the brain's instinct's told you were eating, steak, bacon eggs, ice cream or what ever you wanted to eat etc.

#2

Gary Pepper had inherited a place called Stony Knob, a beautiful place in the Mountains of North Carolina, his Uncle had died, and he was his only living relative, but he didn't know he had one, but was glad because there was a rather large amount of money, and a large home, so he could share with his two children, and there family's, the house was large enough for them all to live there comfortably. But along with that there was a door that Merlin the Magician had created a long time ago, that would open to where ever the owner wanted to go!

#3

Jeffery Martin Hobart, was the grand son, of Sam Adams, who could see into the future, that built his home on top of a Mountain of gold, that only he, Jeff and Mary and of coarse their son Larry, knew it existed, and only one fourth of it had been taken out, Jeff inherited all of it along with a town named Adamsville, there was a textile mill, and he created computer soft ware company, along with pro. teams, Baseball, football, Basketball, a lot people thought he was the richest man in the world, Jeff couldn't see the future like his grandfather, but he and his wife Mary had a child who could see into the future Larry Bobby Hobart, knew everything! Mary's Mother

June was a Graymore, whose family had been around before the Civil War there was a peculiar thing in the Graymore women, they knew their private parts name's Mary's has Nellie, Jeff's has Jake, Larry's has George etc. very strange!!!!!!

CHAPTER 1

Russell Willow, had been a pilot in the Korean War he had graduated from a small junior college, in North Carolina. after his two years, he would have to start looking for the other two years to complete his education, he would have to work and save enough money to go. But he had developed, a good work ethic, and he was sure he could get the money to finish his education.

While working at a machine shop, making decent money, he saw a flyer about becoming a pilot in the Army Air Core. If he could qualify for it, it would be his ticket to school, under the G.I. bill.

So he took all the test to get into the Army Air Core, the next thing he knew he was flying missions in Korea. When it finally ended, he had lost all seven of his buddies, he had made friends with in flight school. So he opted to be discharged out of the Military.

But after seeing all the death and destruction, and the loss of his friends. His mind went into a funk, that took almost a year to work his way through it.

And school was not on his mind, that his life, would be what ever he made it. That there were no magical cures. His family was a joke, he had never been loved by them, he thought that hard work, and patience, would get him through it, in his local area, there was an airport, So he started a business of repairing planes, flight testing. And before long his business grew, and with a crew to help him. He had accumulated enough money, to buy his own plane, it was a beautiful older twin engine prop. He completely restored her, and was using it as a charter service. Which was doing very well.

He bought himself a home, then he started pursuing the ladies, and after five years. He had made love to a lot of women, but he had not fallen in love with any of them. So he decided that he would just let the women he could love find him.

His business had really grown, he had developed a lot of Corp. accounts, that had paid him a lot of money over the years, he had added two Leer Jets to his charter service.

But his first plane, the twin engine, prop, he had a feeling for her, he had rebuilt her several times over the years. But there was something about the drone of the props, purring in his ears. Made him love her more than the new jets, but he couldn't take her home and make love to her, but on occasion while on route to pick up a customer. Ginny, a beautiful young co-pilot/ stewardess would let him put the plane in autopilot and make love to her and to climax at thirty thousand feet, was one of his all time favorite things to do. He felt he was living life on the edge and to the fullest.

Russell Willow was becoming, wealthy and with his adopted brother Bobby Rice handling the business.

He was picking Jobs he wanted to do with his favorite plane, so on a Friday in early may, one of his regular customer groups, called him to charter a round trip to Barbados for a week and half. And Russ was in the mood for a little Island time. He checked the weather charts for the next month and the West Indies looked very good, he negotiated a good price for the trip. They were eight retired school teachers, he took them somewhere every summer, and he had bunked with all of them, they were a fun group of girls, they were all in their late fifties, as was he. He would take his sweet heart, she would hold enough fuel to get them there and half way back and he knew he could refuel in Barbados, so he refitted his plane with retractable pontoons so they could Island hop all they wanted to. He was looking forward to taking this group to the islands.

The weather flying there, was beautiful, the girls were playing games in between napping, the flight was a long trip, but when they finally got there and settled into their quarters at the Hotel. The party started, they wanted to go everywhere, one of the girls, Betsy made them out an itinerary for them to follow. If they were to see every thing on this trip, and they did have a very good time, they drink a little to much, and were silly some times. But Russell was ready to tussle, and did sleep with all of them, he thought Betsy was the most comfortable woman, Susan, the sweetest, Gina, Lola, Martha, Gill, Gail and Sheila were a heck of a lot of fun to sleep with, but before the week and a half was over they had worn him out. He felt he needed a little R. and R. to get over this trip. when it was time to leave, they did so with heavy hearts, but they would remember Barbados for the rest of their lives, they all had a blast. But some of them had family's back home, although they would like to stay forever.

They knew they couldn't so with reluctant hearts they left Barbados.

Russell checked the weather before leaving, he saw a weather front coming toward them that looked pretty bad. But the weather service at the airport in Barbados assured him that he would out run it. All the way to the States so he took off from Barbados.

The weather was just perfect, blue shies and sunny, but with in an hour and a half, the weather or what ever it was had caught up with them. And he was having a hell of a time flying his plane, he tried several times to fly above it but couldn't find any clear skies there, it was all a snarling bitch of a storm.

He was being tossed around and up and down, so he tried another tact, he took her lower, and damn near hit the ocean full force and it scared the hell out of him.

And for a good eight hours it was like riding a roller coaster, up and down until he noticed his fuel gages and they were getting close to empty, all the other instruments seemed to be working fine, Russell knew he was a damn good pilot, and he was flying a damn good plane.

But after flying for ten hours in this crap, he started to worry about the fuel so he started flying lower, hoping that he could find land, he was beginning to think he might just have to land in the ocean.

Which would be death for all of them, but through the flapping blades on his windshield he thought he saw a dark spot to his left, at first it didn't register in his brain, but he knew that was land an headed toward it. when he got closer, he could see what looked like a lagoon and he flew her toward it. He glanced at the fuel gage, he thought it was on empty, and he knew he had only one chance at setting her down, but like the good pilot he was he scooted her perfectly into the Lagoon and stopped. There was what appeared like a mountain in front of them, there was wave action in the lagoon, but after what he had gone through. It was just a gentle rocking of his plane, he knew he had to get out and lash it down. when he got out of his seat, all the ladies looked like zombies, he went to each of them, and assured them that they were finally safe. That he had to get out of the plane and lash it down, when he was through, he got back into the plane he was soaked to the skin.

All the ladies were pulling off his wet cloths until he was naked, they toweled him down, then wrapped him in a warm blanket, his teeth were chattering, when he realized it he started laughing, and that started all of them, when they stopped snickering, Betsy said, "I'm starving," and that started all of them looking for food in the plane, they had stored enough junk food on his plane.

Russell smiled and said, "no wonder we couldn't stay in the air, we were food over loaded, he chuckled, but he thought that could be a good thing now." he said, I'm hungry to," they all started munching junk food when they were full, the wind and rain were still howling, the plane was rocking. They all cuddled together under blankets, in the cockpit, Russell knew that sometime during the night he had climaxed, with somebody, but he didn't know who, that he was so tired, he drifted back to sleep.

And when he roused himself enough to get up, the door to the plane was open, he could hear the girls laughing and playing on the beach of the lagoon. He found his clothes put them on went out and joined them.

He asked "Gail if they had ventured into the foliage?" She said "that they hadn't" he told her, "that was good, he didn't know what kind of animals could be on this Island."

Russell started checking his plane, after checking it over thoroughly he didn't find any damage, he checked the oil in the engine's. It was perfect, he patted her on the side of plane, and said, "that's the way its done old girl, and kissed her on the side of the plane, said "thanks."

He got back into the plane found his guns, he had placed there about a year ago, because he had flown into an airport in up State N. Y. it was late.

And ran into some butt holes who thought they could take his plane. He pulled a monkey wrench from his tool box, when he got through with them, they decided they didn't need his plane after all and ran like hell for safety, because he would die before he would let them have his baby.

He got his handgun and a sawed off shot gun, and shells for both of them, just incase he might need them. He slipped his piece, fully loaded into his pocket, put one round into the chamber of the shotgun and slid in a five round clip into it, made sure the safety was on, got out of the plane.

When the girls saw the gun, they came over to him and asked, "what are you doing with a shotgun Russ?" He smiled and said, "we don't know what kind of vermin live on this island." "I was a boy scout, I want to be prepared for any thing that might come at us."

Shelia said "should we be scared," he said, "no honey, I just want to be ready just in case. Then he asked what have you found for breakfast?"

Betsy said "I had a box of peanut butter crackers and we all had two packs apiece, do you want some?" he smile and said, "my stomach is trying to eat my backbone." They all laughed, she gave him two packs to eat, when he finished eating them, he smiled and said, "its not bacon and eggs, but it sure tasted good."

He asked them "are we ready to check out the Island?" they replied "they were," he told "them all to put on shoes, the ground on the Island could be rough on their feet," with shoes on them all, they followed a small river running into the lagoon, they followed it for an hour, stopped and took a break. While resting,

Lola asked, "has anyone heard any birds, I was wondering if there were any on this Island." Russ replied, "you know I don't think I've ever been on an Island that didn't have birds." Gail said "now that's spooky," when they were rested, they all moved on in what seemed like another hour.

They could hear what sounded like water falling and the closer they got, the louder it sounded, until they walked up to a large crystal clear lake with a water fall coming from the top of the mountain.

Russell said "this must be one of the most beautiful places, I've ever seen, in my life."

And in unison Susan, Gina, Martha, Gill, Lola, Gail, Betsy and Shelia all said "WOW we think your right," he pulled off his shoes, and waded into the water, he cupped his hands and drank. He said, "OK ladies you've got to taste this, it taste like good clean water, its fantastic." Betsy smiled and said "with sweat running down her face, I'm going to do better than that."

She was out of her cloths and jumped into the water naked as a jaybird.

As Russell observed, "WOW" that's not bad looking at all, then the rest followed suit, although he had slept with all of them, he had not seen them naked in the daylight.

And he thought they were truly lovely ladies in any light, they all started playing like children.

Russell got out of the water, put his shoes on, he noticed, what he thought were steps up the side of the mountain he tried them and before he knew it he was looking at where the water was gushing out of the side of the mountain down into the lake below. But what excited him most of all he could see a cave behind the water. He started looking for way into it he walked and crawled all over the top of the mountain. He was wondering how the water was getting up through the mountain to get out where it was coming from. And that's when he found a good size oval hole, about four feet by three feet, he started to crawl into it, then he stopped and thought about the girls, they needed him, to survive this place. Then he pulled out his gun, thought this would give me a fighting chance if he ran into something that wanted to eat him.

He crawled into the cave behind the water fall, he found a large size room, the whole room was covered with moss about an inch thick, it wasn't wet or moist, it felt like carpet.

There was a large round area in the middle of it like a bed, with light coming through the waterfall like a window it wasn't dark at all it felt cozy to him. This place would be ideal in a storm, like the one they had just survived. He walked over to where the water was cascading down into the the lake below, and tried to get the attention of the girls below, but he couldn't so he pulled his cloths off, then he looked to make sure he wouldn't hit any of them, they were clustered to the left of where he would land. So he jumped and made his body into a ball and when he hit the water, there was a big splash. that scared the hell out of the ladies, they screeched loudly but when he came up, Shelia said, "how in the hell did you do that?" Honey I found us a home to live in, he swam to the side of the lake, got out and said follow me ladies to your new home.

They all got out, followed him over to the side of the mountain, he showed them the steps up the side of it, and told them to go up single file. They all started up, Betsy was the last one to go up, she turned smiled and said, "your going to enjoy this aren't you?" He caught her arm, pulled her to him kissed her, and said "you better believe honey pot, he patted her bottom, and he did enjoy the site of all those beautiful butt's climbing up the side of the mountain. when they all got to the top, they were waiting for him, to lead the way, he had to pass them closely, to get by them, and as he did, he kissed each one, and told each one how beautiful they were. When he passed Betsy all the other ladies were giggling and pointed at him. he had developed a nice woody, he smiled and said "sorry ladies, I just can't help it." he told them to follow him, he crawled around to the hole in the rock he went in when they were satisfied that there weren't any crawly thing, they were all in, talking about how nice it was, and started laying down on the mound that looked like a round bed.

One of them said, "beats the heck out of sleeping on the plane," they lay for a good fifteen minutes, giggling at one another, as little girls often do.

Russ said, "should we vote on whether we stay here or at the beach its your choice?"

Betsy said "we would be more comfortable here," Russ, well "we could have our stuff here by night fall, if we hustled." He looked at Betsy, smiled, the others were jumping through the waterfall into the lake to get their stuff from the plane. Russ asked, "Betsy if she would stay for a few minutes, she replied, "yes Russ, I've wanted that damn thing, ever since I saw the woody out side." When the last one was out of the cave, he took her into his arm's kissed her passionately, lifted her and laid her on the mound, and they for a few minutes made love like there was no tomorrow.

When they were satisfied, they held each other feeling the warmth of love making, until Betsy said, "love they will be back up here if we don't get a move on." He got up, picked her up and over to the waterfall, then out they went, when they hit the water, there was big splash, he kissed her under the water and mouthed thanks love. the trip back to the plane, didn't seem as far, as coming up to the lake, he thought about pulling the plane back up to the lake, and asked "what they thought about it," then he thought, wait, "let me check something," he went to the plane, got out a measuring stick, then checked the fuel tanks, and to his surprise, there was about two inches of fuel in both tanks.

He drained the left tank into the right tank, he got out unlashed the plane, then smiled and said "ladies hop on board were going to ride up to the lake with one engine," at first she growled at him, then she sprang to life.

He gently glided her over to the mouth of the river, then started up stream.

On the way, there was a few times, he thought he might have to stop, but there was still enough space for the wings. And in no time they were at the lake, he turned the craft around, to put it closer to the bank, so there cargo wouldn't get wet. Russ told them to wait until, he could lash down the plane before we start unloading." When that was done, it took them a good hour, to get there stuff into the cave, but when that was done the place looked like a cozy room. they all had small folding chairs, Russ brought a steno stove, with six refill cans, he also had a couple of flashlights, so at night the cave wouldn't be pitch black. But he knew, that if they were there for any length of time, those things wouldn't last but a couple of months at best, even with conservation, he would have to come up with a plan to keep them alive.

His plane had been shot down, in North Korean air space, and he was on his own, until he ran into a group of G. I s who were going the wrong way trying to get back to their units, he had been trained to survive if he were shot down. it took them three months, but he lead them all out, they had eaten some horrible stuff but it kept them all alive.

He had made it through that ordeal, thus far this was heaven to him, to be marooned on an Island with eight lovely women, then he wondered how long he would last, trying to satisfy all of them, then he smiled to himself, he would die trying. Then a more somber thought crossed his mind, he had to check the Island out, to find them something to eat, to survive on, he knew the cookies, crackers and candy would run out.

The night came quickly, he lit one of the steno cans, and the room came to life, it was like setting in front of a cozy fire at home with friends.

Betsy passed out the candy bars, they tasted good, he was setting between all eight of them, and there was touching of body parts, by his neighbors Gail and Susan, and with the light flickering in the cave, he finally put his arms around both his neighbors, and was fondling their breast, they were both exciting him, He whispered into "Gail's ear, I'm going out side and in few minutes, you and Susan bring a blanket, I want both of you."

He got up and asked to be "excused, that he had some business to take care of. He assumed they would think he had to take a leak."

But he had more on his mind of a grander nature, for old mother nature, he walked down to the side of the lake with a flash light and waited for them to come down, and in five minutes, they slowly came down the steps.

He pulled them both to him, he could still smell the sweetness of their warm body's he lifted Susan to his standing body and make love to her, until he fell to his knees, they were both laughing with joy.

Gail had spread the blanket, out on the sand, as soon as he was out of Susan he was into Gail and digging for gold they found it quickly.

They lay breathlessly for only a moment, for Susan was ready again.

He was out of Gail then into Susan and the rhythm started again. digging for the gold in earnest passion until it came crashing down, he moaned laid still for a moment. But there was another pair of hands grasping him, so he was out of Susan and into Gail. He thought there was no more gold, but she soon proved him wrong, until he felt a need again, and the digging began with gusto, and that last big thrust there was gold aplenty. All he remembered was them putting their legs across him and he was gone. He didn't know anything until the sun came up and all the other ladies were standing looking at them.

When Betsy saw him open his eye's she said, "that was some business you had last night." "If I had know you were up to this, I would have been here with bells on," he looked up at them and said "I think these two ladies almost killed me last night."

When Gail heard that she and Susan helped him up and threw him into the lake, jumped in behind him, it was all he could do to keep them form drowning him. The girls on the rim of the lake were laughing their heads off so he finally went deeper under the water and swam for the water fall. when he got there, Gail and Susan didn't know where he had gotten to, so he stayed there for a few minutes, to gain his strength, then he crawled from behind the falls. the girl were still looking for him, he snuck back up the steps and into the cave. Put his cloths on, got his shotgun and handgun then went down the other side of the mountain. and started exploring the island, as he got down to the lowlands the foliage wasn't as dense. As on the other side of the mountain, what he found was trees with what looked like eggplants growing and hanging from limbs. they were plentiful, he was hungry, so he picked one from a tree burst it open it smelled just like he remembered eggplants smelling. then the memory of Bo's Mom frying them in a pan, he had always loved eating them.

So he took a bite of it and the strangest thing happened, as he was eating the damn thing, they tasted just like he was eating bacon and eggs, with toast jelly. When he finished eating all of it he was full, and that he had a whole some breakfast, he felt renewed, Then he wondered if he was dreaming, he shook his head, then thought, hell no this was real, so he gathered some of the fruits for the girls.

He took off his knit shirt made a bag out of it, they were so big he could only get six of them in his shirt. And back up the mountain he went, when he got to the cave. He called down to them, when they saw him, they started chewing him out, Lola hollered, "you SOB how did you get up there we were worried sick, you bastard." he walked down to them, opened his shirt showed them what he found.

As they were looking at them, Gina said, "where did you find eggplants?"

Russ replied "on the other side of the Mountain."

He took them to the water edge, washed them off, came back to them and sliced one, and gave each one a good healthy slice, and said take a bite of this. when they started eating, there eyes got big and started smiling, Betsy said

"this taste like a banana split, I can taste the bananas, nuts, chocolate syrup and I just ate the cherry." Then she said "I've been dying for one of these for days."

Then he asked "Shelia, what hers taste like," she said "a good stake, with a baked potato and a fresh baked roll."

They all said "it tasted like something they wanted to eat," four were eating stake with all the trimming, three were eating hamburgers, with fries, with milkshakes. When they had consumed all he brought, he heard a few burps Martha said "are they poison?" Russ said "I have no idea, but if we all die we will be full and happy." then he told them "he thought what ever you wanted to eat, that the egg plant thing or what ever it is, would taste just like it."

So I'm "guessing our minds are telling our taste buds, and we are getting it,"

Gina said "that's impossible."

He laughed and said, "well I just witnessed eight lovely ladies, they were all eating something different."

When I discovered them this morning, and ate one I thought I was eating bacon and eggs with toast and jelly. Betsy asked "if we could get more, if they can do that, I want more, because that was lunch and I will be hungry for supper in a couple of hours." So they rounded up every thing they could carry food in, Russ found a couple of fairly large nets, in the plane, the girls got their pants and tied the legs.

Russ lead the troops, back to where he found the food, they gathered as many as they could, in the assorted vessels they had.

It was a very good haul, when they got back to the cave, Gill wanted to store them under the water to keep them fresh, so they did.

One of them said "if we were home that would be at least three weeks of groceries."

Russ thought now that we have found a food source, he should be thinking about getting off this island.

He spent a few days checking the instruments on the plane. And trying to get a radio signal out to somebody, but none of his efforts worked. he thought he had gotten a mayday signal out before they had to land the plane. then he thought about the storm, and when he considered where and how they got here, he thought they were damn lucky to be alive, he thought if only he could get some fuel, they could get the hell out of here. So after a couple of nice days, some very nice visits from Martha, Gill and Betsy.

He was resigned to his fate. which from where he was looking, he had all the body fluids he needed.

So he gave up on the plane for now, when he got back to the lake the girls were taking turns jumping from the cave through the water fall.

He was simply admiring their bodies, they were mature ladies, the only one of them was a little on the plus size was Betsy, but she was simply delicious to have sex with.

Watching them his body started responding, he thought how can this be, after last night, but it was fun with those two.

By the time he got up to the lake he had a full blown woody, he dropped his pants, pulled off his shirt and dove into the lake. the first one he got to was Gill, she's is a very charming girl, he did the back stroke around her, when she noticed what was sticking out of the water he smile at her and said "would you like to."

She smiled back at him and said "would I ever she pulled him down and into her." (talk about the motion of the ocean) they were making waves.

When the others saw what was going on. Lola swam over to them and said "I'm next, when she thought Gill had enough." She pulled him around and into her, there were more waves, maybe even a tidal wave, when they were finished.

He said "no more, the twins can't handle anymore, he swam to the shore and quickly got out of the water, and put his cloths on."

He looked at Shelia, Martha, and Gina, "later you beautiful ladies," he went over to the stash of food, got one, started eating, it tasted like corn beef with mash potatoes, slaw and a wedge of peach pie, he was hungry, but it was gone in a flash. he could feel his body being energized, and it radiated through him, he felt refreshed. by that time it was getting dark, he thought of the three girls, he smiled to him self just maybe.

They were all in the cave when the sun finally set, but there was a glow that lingered for a good thirty minutes, that was almost magical in the way it reflected off the girls, they seemed to look younger, even Betsy looked thinner, but she still looked delicious.

When he got into the cave, someone had already lit a steno can, and the glow of it was dancing off the walls. they were all naked, and laying on the bed he asked "I'm I getting to sleep with you girls or do I sleep on the floor."

They all smiled and one of them pointed to the middle of the bed, he smiled and said "that sounds like fun," he dropped his shorts, and crawled into the middle of the bed, there were hands pulling and tugging at his body, he knew what was in store for him.

When he lay on his back, it was already standing tall, they all scooted closer to him. he smiled and said "why do I feel like I'm going to be attacked, Gina giggled and said "because you will be, we drew straws for you and I'm first do you have a problem with that."

He smiled and said "not at all honey," when he said "that the fray began with Gina, he was into her, quickly, he didn't want to start digging, he wanted to enjoy the feeling and the texture of being in side her warm soft body." but he could tell she wanted the deed to began, so he gave her what she wanted and the digging started in earnest.

He could feel hands all over his bottom, helping with the rhythm of the deed at hand, when they were both ready the gold it happened.

Before he knew it he was into Shelia, she wanted the gold right away so he started digging quickly until they found the gold.

There was no pause, because Martha had him inside her body quickly and she wanted lots of digging, her gate was slower, but her needs were greater, he could tell when she was ready for the gold and it came quickly.

And before the night was over, he was into the rest of them, and he did Betsy twice.

He felt he could do them all again, but sleep had overtaken them all, and he drifted into dream land himself.

When he did wakeup, the cave was empty, when he didn't hear voices or laughter like the previous mornings.

He felt concerned, he got out of bed, pulled on a pair of shorts and shoes found his weapons, his shotgun was missing, but the handgun was still there.

He wondered if they were capable of firing the shotgun so he hurried out of the cave to look for them, they were not visible anywhere, not in the lake.

He walked down to the lake and called for them, he got no response, and that gave him a scare, he thought where could they be? Then he thought about firing his gun, into the air to see if he could get a response.

And he did, it sounded like it came from the beach, so he headed that way, when he got there he saw them coming toward him.

He saw their footprints going up the beach, and knew they had walked around the Island.

When they got to him, he told them they should have informed him of their trek around the Island, you gave me a scare, I didn't know what could have happened to all of you. Betsy replied "honey we all thought you should rest, after last night." he smiled and said "you girls were all asleep before I was finished."

Betsy laughed and said "we all thought you would be tired this morning."

He hugged each one of them, and said "don't do that again, or you just might get a spanking."

Martha laughed then said "now that might be interesting," he smiled then said "just kidding love."

He asked "them how far did go on your quest of the Island?" Gina said "we came down on the other side of the river, and started walking that way, she pointed to their footprints going up the beach, and walked all the way around, it's a good six miles around."

We were looking for other human beings, Betsy who had the shotgun said "we didn't want to run into any wild things, so I thought we might need this," she held the shotgun up, he asked, "her if she had ever fired one of those things?" yes she replied "my ex-husband like to shoot skeet, and I tried to bond with him before the divorce, but it pissed him off that I could shoot skeet better than he could."

Russ said "that's good to know, has anyone else had any dealing with fire arms?" they all shook their head, no, he looked at Betsy and said "you young lady are in charge of that firearm."

She replied "well Russ, this isn't a skeet gun, this is a sawed off shotgun, there is a big difference."

He replied "I know honey, but if needed, at close range it will shred anything that comes at you, and that's my main concern right now."

By the way did you see any animal tracts, or any birds?" They replied no then he said "do you know how strange that is."

"Most of the inhabited islands, humans being have brought with them, animals and birds."

"I can only assume we are the first humans, to find this place in the ocean,"

Shelia said "what do you mean?" Well honey, "we could be stranded here, if there are no shipping lanes and no flights over us, we may not be found. none of my equipment is working, on the plane, there is a beacon on it but I don't think its working."

By that time they were setting on the beach, looking worried he thought he could see tears forming in their eyes.

Russ said "look we've survived what could have been a horrible death in the ocean, we've found a beautiful place."

"That will keep us alive and you girls look younger to me, I know we are the same age."

"But after only three days you are all looking like ice cream Sundays to me and I do love ice cream Sundays."

He chuckled, that seemed to change their mood, then he asked? "what they all had for breakfast, they all were different. Then he told them he had not eaten yet, that he wanted to find them first.

He was worried about them. (he sang) (all alone and feeling blue and no one to tell my troubles to, remember me I'm one who loves you)" they seemed to like that, he did love them all. three days turned into six months, during the day they stayed busy, looking over the Island, and building communal huts for them all to stay in, but most of the time they stayed in the cave, it became home to them, it was warmer at night, they would cluster together and every night he would make love to them all.

Then he started wondering, if any them would get pregnant, he thought he would like that, he had no children of his own.

He knew he had spread enough semen to them all, that if they were going to get pregnant, it would have already happened.

They all ran around the Island in the mornings, and some kind of work to keep minds busy, and would run around in late afternoons, it seemed to Russ that they were getting younger.

They were all becoming beauty queens to him, but he was partial to them all they made his boat float and float often, he had lost his stomach and his and his floating device had grown, he didn't know if it was the frequent use of it or the food and water they were consuming.

But none of the ladies had any complaints, he found what he thought was oil seeping out of the ground.

It was useable for burning, on the torches, they used at night in the cave, it lit up the cave as bright as any lighting system as he could remember.

But he knew he hadn't seen any electrical lighting in a very long time, and it made the cave warm, for their naked body's, they were never in cloths at night, during the day they did wear something, but Russ, could always see what ever he wanted.

And the six months, turned into a year, Russ, thought that all of them were mentally adjusted to their fate, in Paradise, he knew it was for him, with eight beautiful women that wanted him, could a fellow ask for more.

During the day one or two would come to him and want a session at one of the huts. that always turned out to be a heck of a party, for him, today it was Betsy and Gail's turn, they had already gone, to the beach, he was to show up when the sun was over his head, then he left all the girls knew what was going on, for all he knew they had planned it.

When he got to the hut, they were frolicking in the ocean, he didn't like them playing in the ocean, he had told them about sharks, they had never seen any, but he was leery of them.

When he saw them playing in the ocean, he started chewing "them out, until they came out of the water." the sun glistening off their breast, and hips, when they got to him, Betsy was shaking her head and smiling, he knew he had to have her right then.

He picked her up and was into her, on the beach, until their needs were met, he dropped to his knees, laughing with joy, he kissed her mouth and her breast.

Until Gail let him know that she was ready to, Betsy and he got up went into the ocean and rinsed the sand off their body's.

They walked back up to Gail, he pulled her to him, kissed her and the woody began, she said "not in the sand love," he lead them both into the hut, before they had fully gotten Into the room.

Gail had rapped her legs around him, she had him inside of her, he smiled kissed her passionately, dropped to his knees.

And the digging began in earnest, she was churning and he was burning, until they both found that special place.

Betsy pulled him away from Gail, and he was into her, Betsy was special to him, he wasn't sure just why, but he thought he loved them all, but then they found that special zone, and they melted together.

Gail rolled him over and into her and she was off to the races, for a few moments, he was just along for the ride, until he felt the need coming on, and they both found it together.

When he rolled over he pull them both close to him and for a few minutes they lay in the warmth of love.

Gail went to sleep, with a gentle snore, she was sleeping peacefully, and he started to drift off, when Betsy reached for his package and it came to life he rolled over and into her.

She was truly a delicious lady to make love to, when they were through and had revived themselves.

He took them, with him, to the oil pond, to make more torches, after he made a dozen.

He asked "Betsy and Gail if any of them had taught science or chemistry in school."

That "he was sure this was crude oil and if we could figure out how to convert this into fuel for the plane.

And if we could make enough fuel, we could get off this Island."

Russ had kept up the maintenance on his plane, he had used some of the oil from the pit to keep his plane lubricated, he turned the prop over as often as he could, and he felt like his baby would fly, if only she had fuel.

Gail said "honey we are all from Texas, and our folks were in the oil business." "So among all eight of us we could figure out how to make fuel for the plane."

They took the torches back to the cave, Betsy started, "asking if any one could remember how to refine crude oil," Shelia said "I sure do, my Dad worked in a refinery," "but I'm not sure we could do it here, it's a long process as I remember."

Russ asked "her if she thought we could rig something up here on the Island."

That "if we could figure out how to do it, even if it takes a long time, we do have lots of time, on our hands." They all got excited about the idea, that they could leave this place, and started thinking about what they needed to do the job.

With in a months time, they had worked out a plan, and started refining the oil on the Island. it was very crude, but as Russ could remember, it was much like making moon shine.

But it worked, and they were making thirty gallons of fuel a month, and to Russ it looked, smelled and tasted like the fuel that was left in his plane, And they were straining it through an old pair of Betsy's cotton panties, before they put it into the plane.

She said "its got to be grade A-# 1 to go through her panties," and Russ could vouch for that, because he knew just what was in her panties and it was grade A#1 stuff.

After three months, they had ninety gallons, in the planes tanks, and with another ninety gallons, the plane would be fully loaded.

So he asked "if they wanted to take a ride, to try out the fuel, and they all wanted to go."

He got them all into the plane, he turned the props over, they sputtered at first, but then came to life, it was a sweet solid drone of sound that was music to his ears, he patted the instrument panel, and said thanks love you still got it.

He gently turned down stream, when he got to the Lagoon, he lined her up to go through the entrance of the lagoon.

He turned to the girls, and said "cross your fingers ladies, revved up the engine's" and they were in they air before they left the Lagoon.

Russ gently turned her to the left and climbed to a thousand feet into the air and flew around the Island. she handled beautiful, he flew out a little further, then around again he asked the girls to check for reef's or sand bars.

Then he lowered the plane to five hundred feet so they could see better and went around twice.

And no one saw any signs of reefs or sandbars, Russ thought, to him self that a boat or a good size ship could dock on the Island.

With out any difficulty, and that brought the question to his mind, why had nobody found this place, was it so far off the beaten path, of mankind that he could claim it for his own.

That sent a thrill through his mind, thinking that this Island could be his, he fantasized the name (Russell's) or (Willow's) island.

He decided on (Willow's Island), then he thought that was all wishful thinking.

And with out the girls, this place would be lonely as hell, so he thought he better get back to business.

That it would be three more months, to get enough fuel.

Then someone kissed him on his ear, and said "what are you thinking about Russell Willow."

Then he realized it was his Betsy, the sweet sent of her body, he reached around and pulled her into his lap, and started kissing her lips, and her breast, as she sat on his lap she felt the wood in his pants, she whispered into his ear, "you think we could".

He thought seriously about having her right now, then he decided, they would waste to much fuel.

So he kissed her deeply and said "later love, but I'm having you before you get off this plane."

He brought his plane back down into the lagoon, and taxied her back up to the lake. When the rest of the girls got off the plane and he had lashed it down, he had his Betsy twice.

The next three months, seamed to drag along, because they knew they would be leaving.

But there was some sadness about, leaving to, this had been their home they were happy here, all their wants and needs had been taken care of by Russ, he was the leader of their pack.

When the plane was finally full of fuel, on a Monday, they were all debating when they would leave, and none wanted to leave until the weekend.

Russ was being called on more than usual, for their sexual needs, it was fine with him, because each time he made love, it was always better then the time before. They packed the plane the night before, with food and water and their worn cloths.

Russ was telling them that things will have changed, and that we are probably dead, to all the loved ones we knew.

It's been a good two years, and it will probably shock them all when they see us alive. But what I would really like to say to all of you, I love you all, I wish you would come and stay with me.

CHAPTER 2

As they flew away from the island. Russ, thinking to himself, he would be back, to this beautiful place, remembering all the love they had shared here together. the girls had left a sign on the island that read (Willow Island) and that made Him feel proud inside.

Instead of growing older together they had grown younger together. When they arrived on the island they were all in their fifties. And as they were flying away, they were all in there thirty's, he had Betsy to get samples of the water and the purple fruit (eggplant) is all he could think of to call it, because to him that's what it looked like.

He was thinking that they might just have found the fountain of youth and with the sweet crude oil on the island, he was sure it would be worth trying to claim it as their own, and would do so as soon as they got back to civilization.

He felt they all were just a little sad to be leaving. For two years that had been their home. But little did he know, what he would be confronted with when they were back to the Carolina's.

Russ had plotted the latitude and longitude. He was sure he could find his why back to their paradise.

As he was flying across the Florida Keys, he thought about landing and checking his plane out, but she was purring like a Kitten. he and the ladies were to excited about going home. He thought, they would be there in about two hours.

When they circled the airport in Gastonia, he radioed his call letters for landing instruction. And what came back was an excited voice "asking him to repeat, his call letters again please." Russ did, "is that you Rusty?" yes Bobby! "his reply was damn! Its good to hear the sound of your voice, boy do we have a lot to talk about!" his reply was Bob I'm sure we do. Bob said "the runway is clear come on in." when they taxied up to the hanger all the guys in the Shed came running out and looking over the plane and putting shocks under the wheels.

Russell opened the doors, and was helping all the ladies out of the plane. when they were all out and on the tarmac he noticed that their cars were gone from the parking lot where they had left them he turned to Bob and "ask what happened to our rides?" Bob pulled him away form the plane and with a grim look on his face he explained "Rusty you Dad died three months after we thought you had died at sea. You mom remarried some Dud, his name is Chester Potts, he showed up not long after you went missing. And he has bugged the hell out of me trying to find out just how much money she was entitled to from your business, I've ran him off from here a number of times, once I caught him in the office looking threw the files and I physically escorted

him out the door. I went to the bank and talk to Dick about
keeping an eye on him, I told him that I thought the man was
a crook, we decided to set you mother up with an account that
we could monitor how she was spending the money. Dick set her
up with a fifty thousand dollar checking account. She or he has
gone through half million dollars. Your mom sold her old house
and moved into your place and that's where they are living now,
your car was traded for a Corvette and at your mother's age, she
looks foolish riding around town but we wanted her to be happy.
Gina's car was picked up by her family they showed me their I.
D. so I let them take it. Because we thought you all were dead.
Betsy's van no one came looking for it and we've been using it
around the business, its in good shape. Sorry Rusty, "but you're a
rich man, and I know you will straiten this all out."

"Yes Bobby I will, and thanks for taking care of our business,
but right now I'm tire and I know all the girls are to, so lets get
them inside and try to get them in touch with their family's."
when Rusty came back from talking to Bobby, he started trying
to get the girls into the office. So they could call their family's.

Betsy saw that Gina's car was gone, but hers was still there she
turned to Rusty and told him about Gina's car being gone. He
smiled and said, "honey mines gone to, don't worry we still got
your ride." With that she kissed him and said "we wont have to
walk will we" Rusty chuckled and said

"your with me baby, and I know you won't walk anywhere
with out me."

Bobby had gotten the ladies somewhat comfortable.

And all the girls were calling their family's and one by one they were not getting in touch with anyone the numbers had all been changed Rusty saw that they were beginning to look worried, so he decided to talk to to them, he told "them to remember they have been gone for two years. And most likely were considered dead. So lets all go to my house and rest up overnight, and tomorrow surely things will look better," he turned to Betsy I think "we can all get in your van," he turned to Bob asked him "to get in touch With their Lawyer, about getting us all back into the land of the living and ask him how one goes about claiming and Island? That's where we've been living for the last two years."

Bob wanted to ask him all about their adventure. But Rusty smiled and said "Bobby I'll tell you all about it when were all rested," he turned to the girls and said "I think we all can get into Betsy's van, so lets all head over to my my place and get some rest."

When they pulled into Rusty's driveway, there was a sporty new Corvette setting in the driveway, he and all the girls got out and walked to the door he rang the doorbell and his mother opened the door, she said yes! Russell asked "how are you Mrs. Willow?" she looked at him and said that's not my name anymore, a man came and stood behind her then she said "get away from my door," and slammed it shut, Russell looked at the girls and said "I "don't think were welcome at my house."

Just as they started loading up the van, a police car pulled in behind them and a cop got with his hand on his gun, until he saw who it was, "Russell Willow we all thought you were dead" Bo Arrow what are you doing here they hugged each other, Bo "said its been a long time sense we were in diapers together".

Rusty replied "you bet it has, lets go to you car, tell me why you are here?"

Your Mother call and said "there was a bunch of strange people trying to get into her house." Dam that bitch, Russ said, "that's my house!" "Bo can we call Bobby on your system?" "Sure he replied, he picked up his mike and called the dispatcher," thread him through to Bobby at the Work Shack when Bobby answered, Bo said "the boss wants to talk to you", and passed the mike to Rusty, Bob call "Dick at the bank and tell him to cut Mrs. Potts off from any more of my money, she can have what's in her account now but that's it, at least for now!"

I couldn't get into my house, can you take care of that for me, "sure Rusty consider it done" and by the way I'm taking the girls up to the Comfort Suites on Remount Rd. we need to get some rest, we will need some, money you got any on hand, Bob replied, "if you still got your check card its still good." damn! let me check, yes I do, thanks Bob, "if you need to get in touch with me call the front desk, they will buzz me, but give me at least a good 12 hours, oh and if you can get my plane checked out, pull the crew from the Work shack I'll probably have to fly the girls home to Waynesville when they get over the shock of being back. Oh and check the fuel for sure that's something the girl's and I cooked up on the island. To get our butts back home I know you must have a lot of questions, but if we can claim the

Island For ourselves we'll have some of the sweetest crude oil that I've ever seen.

See you in about 12 to 13 hours and thanks." He thank "Bo, for getting Bobby on the horn for him," Bo looked at him, and said "Rusty Willow when you set down with Bobby and tell him your story, I want to be there to, you with all those beautiful ladies, for two years, I've got to hear that tale to" Rusty smiled, "when I do if you can keep it just between us, its a deal." "Rusty you got a deal"! When they got to the Hotel, Comfort Suites Bobby had already booked, their rooms, and after showers they were in bed, Rusty didn't know how long he had sleep, but sometime during his sleeping Betsy had crawled into his bed and they had made love, he didn't know how long, but they went right back to sleep, the next thing he knew he was being fondled by Gina, then she got on top of him and rode like a horse and he enjoyed the whole experience, she whispered into his ear, "I woke up and Betsy was gone, and knew just where she was so I decided it was my turn."

When he roused himself the next morning. All eight of them were in bed with him, Susan, Lola, Martha, Gill, Sheila and Gail and he had made it with all of them. They all made did group hug, and Rusty said "we could all Move to Salt Lake and become Mormons." They all chuckled over over that!

Gail said "we need to go shopping for something to wear I'm out of panties and I don't think they'll let me go around naked, on the island

It was a lot of fun, watching Russ go around with his bodacious pointer sticking out." Russell smiled at them all. And said "I am only human my Sweet cakes."

"If you girl's want to go shopping, we had better, get a move on, I was thinking you would want to fly up to Waynesville and check on your condos to see if they've been sold or what the status is?"

When Russ finally got them out of the Westfield Mall they were loaded down with packages and giggling like little girls as little girls often do, but he had also gotten quite a few things to, he was thoroughly enjoying being with the loves of his life. they were happier today than they were yesterday, so he felt good for them he hoped things would turn out ok for them all, he knew he would try his very best To make it so. when they got back to the Hotel, and put on some of the thing they bought, they wanted to go out somewhere and eat. He called Bobby and asked "him where's a good place to eat." Bobby told "him about the

Olive Garden, and its just down, New Pope rd. from where your staying,

I always enjoy eating there". he loaded up the ladies and they found it, and they all eat to much. As they were leaving, a guy approached Rusty and told him he was a "reporter for the Gaston Gazette news paper, he said "Bobby called him and told him that you were back." We ran the story about you disappearing, with eight

School teachers on board your plane, and after three months of searching that you were all assumed dead." "My name is Leo

Heart" they shook hands Russell turned to the ladies and asked if they wanted to talk to the press about their adventure on Willow's Island. they said "they would, then Betsy looked at each of the girls and said "we could talk to him, and omit some of the things that happened there."

Rusty smiled at them and said my lips are sealed. "I love each one of you!" and put his hand on his heart then zipped his lips. He turned to Leo and said "we can talk in the lobby of the hotel were staying at for a while, the Comfort Suiets on Remount rd. were going back now if you want to follow us," he replied "sure I'll see you in about ten to fifteen minutes." they were in the lobby of the hotel, Leo came in and shook hands with each of the girls they told him their names, "Betsy Hope, Susan Dobson, Gina Miller, Lola Albright, Martha Thather, Gill Summers, Gail Holt and Sheila houser."

Leo set them all down in the lobby of the hotel, and got them all what ever they wanted to drink, and started interviewing, he told them "they looked really good after being marooned on a deserted island for two years!" the girls told him "the island wasn't that bad we found all the things we needed to survive and after the first few months we began to enjoy being there and that Russell being an ex military man knew how to survive he Showed us how to live and be happy."

And of coarse did not talk about their love life there. When Leo got through with the interview, he took pictures of them, Russ walked out with him and Leo turned and looked at Russ and said "you on an Island with all those very lovely ladies, I know you had a very good time, Russ smiled at him, said, "you my friend will never know just how good it was!" the reporter looked at him, and said I know theres is a damn good book

In your experiences on an Island with all those beauties. And if you need any help with wrighting it let me know. Russell smiled at him and said "I might just take you up on that offer." That is if the girls would let me do it! Leo said "the title would be living in Paradise." As he walked away he said this "will be front page news tomorrow, and will probely be picked by the wire services." when he walked back into the Hotel the girls "wanted to know what else he told him," Russ held up his hand and said you know I would never talk "about us because I love you all, and to me you are very, very special and what we have is between us. Oh yes Leo said our story would be front page News tomorrow, they all seemed pleased about that." as they were walking back to their rooms, Russ told them that he would call Bob to see if the plane was good to go for their trip tomorrow. They all looked at him, then Betsy said "we don't know wheather were ready to face that just yet! And we don't have to do we!" He pulled them all into a huddle. "You tell me when we go OK." that seamed to please them, as they were walking away, Russ held Betsy hand, "you young lady are staying with me, and as soon as we can I want to make it legal," she smiled said "Russell I'm staying with you weather its legal or not." He opened the door and pulled her into his room, and the night was all theirs. When they woke up the next morning, all the girls were setting on their bed. "Gill greeted them with good morning you two. The Girls and I decided that we should all go to Waynesville. And get it over with, if they've sold our homes, they owe us bigtime, we all had healthy bank accounts. That there would be enough money for us to start over if we have to, and by the way Mr. Willow we all came to your room expecting some cuddle time with you. But Betsy had you in a vice grip and wouldn't let go, we tried to move her, she wouldn't move!"

Susan "said we shouldn't try, that you two looked good together, but that doesn't mean we'll stop trying to."

Russ looked at Betsy and said "what do you think love." Well we've always sheared you, I care a lot for my friends, so I think it shouldn't change now."

Well ladies I guess were going to Waynesville, its eight o'clock, what time do you want to leave here? Betsy looked at them, Gail said "why not, as soon as we can get ready!" Russ took a quick shower, and called the Work shed. when Bobby answered the phone, Russ said "good morning Mr. Rice. he laughed and said "good morning to you Boss, Rusty your plane checked out just fine, the fuel was grade A I put it all back in and just added to the tanks, we cleaned it up, and checked it from one end to the other and couldn't find anything wrong with your Baby." Russ replied "you should have been with me during that damn freakish storm, she road it like the lady She is, the only thing, she just ran out of fuel. before I start talking to much Bob have my plane ready this morning, the girls want to fly up to Waynesville, I'm assuming there's an airport or will I have to fly into Ashville?" Well Rusty "I'll have to check on that I don't know but when you get here

I'll have you a flight plan, by the way I put a Global Positioning gizmo on your plane, I'm surpised you didn't already have one, we could have found you any where on the planet and this time I'm going to know where your butt is at all times, Mr. Willow!" Rusty laughed said "thanks Bobby I guess somebody needs to look out for me, that's what good friends are for."

Thanks again Bobby, as soon as I can round up the ladies, we'll see you!

He hung up the phone, when he saw they were all ready, he got them In the van. They were at the airport, with in twenty five minutes, Bob gave "Russ his flight plan, the G.P.S. location of the Waynesville airport, he told him "its probably the size of Gastonia's airport, and you have a beautiful day to fly," He looked at the girls told them. "He hoped ever thing up in the Hills would be good for them, and helped them get into the plane, he took Russ's hand and said "I'll be watching you Rusty Willow, be safe."

When Russ shut the door of the plane he looked at the girls, and said "we are ready for this right?" Then helped Each of them buckle up, with hug's and a kiss's, he put Betsy in the co-pilot seat.

They were in the air, quickly, the sky was bright and clear. Russ felt good to be back in the air again, he hoped things would be alright, for the girls in Waynesville, then he thought, about the Island, then he asked Betsy "about the samples she had gotten on the Island, she smiled said I gave them to Bobby, he said he would sent them to the closest lab in the Area to analyze and would let me know what they found."

Russ chuckled and said "we've been putting a lot on Bobby lately, but he's a very smart guy and I'm sure he can handle it."

Betsy said "isn't it beautiful up here today," Russ smiled and said "I thought about you and I having a go at it, but I don't think we have the time and the girls would let us get a way with it in front of them," she smiled and said "sounds like fun though, mabe another time."

He patted her knee, you better belive it Babe, they were over Forest City,

Spindle and Rutherford in no time, then over Ashville, he told "Betsy were going to be there soon," he picked up the mike and radioed "the tower in Waynesville he was approaching their airport," there response was "yes Mr. Willow we were expecting you, a Mr. Rice told us to take care of you. come on in there nothing in front of you," he circled and came in from the west and landed his craft like the pro he was, he taxied his plane where they told him to park, when he cut his engins and opened the door and a van pulled to the plane, Russ helped the ladies out of the plane. The driver shook his hand, and introduced himself as "Sam Parks, Bobby and I are good friends, I read about you'all in the paper this morning. So I know about the ladies, living here, Bob did some research, and told me where To take you all," Russ said thanks "Sam, I know we were in the dark as where to start, so lets get started."

Sam drove them to a gated community, he stoped at the office, they got out when they got into the office, a lady setting at a desk, looked sheepishly at them and at a man setting in a chair.

When the man saw Russ he got up and introduced himself as "Art Moore a lawyer form Ashville, Bobby called me to meet you here in case I was needed, I've already talked to people who built the condos, and keep the maintenance up in the community what they did isn't against the Law, but come with me Bill Lay is in the conference room, he will explain," they all gathered around the table, after each one shook his hand, and "he apologized to each of them, we though you all had died at sea!

Mrs. Hope, Mrs. Miller, Mrs. Albright, Mrs. Dobson, Mrs. Summers, and Mrs. Thather your places have only been leased, they couldn't be sold for a period of time, not until you were declared dead.

He looked at there Lawyer, Art shook his head yes! Bill said "Your cars and furniture are in storage, we used some of the money to pay for storage and the rest we put in an account for each you."

Then he looked at Mrs. Holt and Mrs. Houser, "I'm sorry to have to tell you that your husbands sold your places after six months when they declaired you missing, so we have no responsibility to you other than that we are very sorry That this happened to you."

Shela and Gail looked at each other, Gail said "do you have phone numbers and addresses for these good fellow's?" Bill smiled at them and handed each a card, "I think this is all you'll need, to get in touch with them."

"Now for the rest of you, your homes have gained in value, you bought them for two hundred and fifty thousand Dollars, now they are worth four hundred seventy five thousand dollars each. The people who are occupying your places are good people, but if you want your homes back, we have no other recourse but to evect them, but if you want to sell them I'm sure these people would buy them at the going rate, so the decision is yours! I know you don't deserves all this crap, after all you been through, but fate has laid it in your hands. So you will have to tell us what you want us to do?"

Rusty looked at his watch, then said "it close to lunch time, lets all go get something to eat, and talk this over, Art you come with us and help us through this maze."

Art got them in a private room at the restaurant. When they were through Eating Russ ask "what they wanted to do, Betsy said she would like to Sell hers, that she didn't want to live there anymore," so one by one they all wanted to do the same. Russ said "combined you ladies will have two Million almost three, and that is security, worth having."

Then he looked at Gail and Shela, we are a family and family's comes first so whatever comes you way comes ourway, he looked at all the girls and they all said "yes in agreement."

Shela and Gail got phones put in front of them, they called their former husbands When they got through talking to them, Shela told "them what Frank said "he had saw the story in the paper, and was truly sorry but that he had remarried, and that he had two children with his new wife, and he wouldn't leave her and had hired a lawyer, for a divorce! And he would meet with her for the divorce proceeding, anywhere she liked," she told him to meet her at twelve o'clock at the hotel they would be staying at, and gave him the address," she hung up the phone.

Gail said "Larry told her he had seen the papers, and was sorry but he had remarried and that he and his new wife had a child together and he wanted a divorce," she "told him to meet with her tomorrow with a lawyer at twelve noon and gave him the address" she whispered sob as she hung up the phone she looked around the room and said "sorry."

They all laughed and Betsy said "you go girl," Gail and Shela look at Art and said "your going to help us out here aren't you?" Russ looked at him "As I understand Mr. Moore your commeted to us for as long as we need you?" that's right Mr. Willow, for as long as you need me, I gather you all want to sell your holding in the housing, what about the storage things the cars and furniture? Betsy looked at the other girls, and ask, "there might be somethings that we want to keep. I know I want to go back into my condo before we sell, there is a hidden vault that I was stashing away for the future. I knew Ray was about to scoot, so I was prepairing for my future. She smiled and looked at Russ, he's the guy I told you about, the skeet shooting dud."

Russ smiled and said "I remember love! I guess you all want to look at the stuff in storage, they all seemed to agree, he looked a Art and said "lets get started with the paper work to sell the condos, let the ladies look to and see if There's any thing they want to keep."

Art said we need to prepare for Gail's and Sheila's encounter with their Ex. husbands, he looked at them, and said remember they sold your property they both looked at each other, and replied "is there anyway to get inform—ation on their financial status? With kids we don't want to be mean to them," but if its there we want it. Art said "I'll check into it and let you know tomorrow." Russ told "him that they would be staying in town at a local hotel, and he would take care of the meeting rooms at the hotel for their meeting, and if you want to stay with us I'll check you in also," he replied no "I'll go back to Ashville, there I can check on the ex husbands bank Accounts we have a networking group that can do that with out stepping on anybody's toe's, and I'll call the condo's group and get them started with that paper work, and tell them about Mrs. Hope wants to go into her place to get something she's left there. I'll see you in the morning around ten o'clock, you have a good day!" as Mr. Moore, walked from the room, "Russ asked the ladies, where are we Spending the night?" Gill said "we have a Comfort Suites here in town and we like the one in Gastonia, so lets stay there, Betsy picked up one of the phones on the table, and they had a place to stay, she told "them she could only get three suites, she looked at Russ and smiled, is that ok for you Mr. Willow? he picked her up off the floor and said "if its ok for you Mrs. Willow, you know its ok with me love!"

When he did that all the ladies started fussing at Betsy, "you had him last its our turn!" Betsy smiled at them, "did you hear what he called me, my good friends. He called me Mrs. Willow, but I think we are all Mrs. Willow to him, Russ smiled and shook head yes." when they checked into the comfort Suites, all there rooms were adjoining after they got showered and dressed, it was five thirty and they were all hungry, when Russ came into the room, he asked them "where are we going to eat?" Betsy said "do you like Chinese we use to have a good one. Mrs. Willow wants some, and some Chinese food to and winked at him, he smiled then said "I think I'm ready for whatever come's love. And they all went to a very good Chinese restaurant, talk and laughed for two hours about living on the island, and before they left they were all, feeling a little lonely about being a way form home. This was their third day home and though things were moving smoothly, it was still a hassle to them!

When the people at the restaurant started acting funny they finally got message, they wanted them to move on, they left a fourty dollar tip, and "thanked all the help."

When they got back to the hotel, they all gathered in Russ's room, watched some television, until Russ told them that "Art would be here at ten o'clock and you ladies need to be ready, for what ever comes. Now lets all get naked and have some fun, who's first," Russ had a very good night he went to sleep around three in the morning, just looking at all there beautiful body's!

He wondered just how long, he would be able to make love to all of them, knowing that the laws of the land, would not permit him to enjoy them forever, unless they were back on the island, but he didn't know even after a few months if they would even want his love.

That reminded him of an old saying, (make hay while the sun is shining) he chuckled to himself, he would damn sure keep trying.

He was sure he would marry Betsy she pleased him in every way, and she gave him a good feeling in his heart.

The girls didn't wake him until nine o'clock, when he roused himself, he asked "Betsy why she hadn't pushed him out of bed, she kissed him "well love you were at it all night and we all thought you needed the rest!" He showered, shaved and was ready before Art got there, he went to the Hotel office and they showed him the offices he could use for their meeting's.

When Art got there he showed him the offices they would be using, Art said "they were fine, and that he had checked on the financial status of Frank

Houser, Larry Holt and he was pleased to announce that they would be able to Pay back what they received for their former wives property, which by way was three hundred thousand, if they are reluctant to give it back, there is a lot of crap we can dump on the heads.

So I think we shouldn't have any problems with them, and I have the paper work for selling their condos, and as soon as they're signed I have cashiers checks for each one of them."

Russ said "Art you are one damn good lawyer, I figured it would take at least A good week and a half to get this all done."

Gail and Sheila walked up to them and told them that there "ex's had just pulled into the parking lot."

Art looked at his watch then said "there just a tad early I've got eleven forty," he looked a Russ and "asked what time do you have?" "the same as as you councilor, then Russ smiled and said "those guy's aren't really married to the women they're living with are they?" Art smiled and said "that's the reason I don't think we will have any problems with them." the two men with their lawyers walked into the lobby of the Hotel and the desk clerk escorted them to where they were, when the ex's saw their ex Wifes they began stareing at them, Art saw this and said "watch it fellows your tongue's are hanging out, and at this stage you don't get to do that any More!"

Art showed them which office to go to, he got them seated, and asked Gail And Sheila if they wanted to go in one at a time, Gail said "that's how she wanted to do it and it was alright with Sheila," so he took each one into the meeting room and they were out in twenty minutes, when the girls got back with their friends they showed them the checks they had gotten from their Ex's they were happy, three hundred thousand each, Sheila said you know what that a-hole said to me, "Sheila you are a beautiful woman, how did you Manage that on a deserted island."

Gail laughed and said "Larry couldn't keep his eyes off of me, I thought about giving him the finger, but after I saw the amount of the check I just didn't look at him anymore."

Russ smiled and said "you ladies are now divorced, you can marry me!"

Art came back and told the, "others to come with him, he wanted them to sign the sellers contract's, and he would give them their checks to." One by one they were all taken care of, he told Betsy he was giving her check now but she could go into her condo, and collect from the hidden vault and the storage items, I have receipts to get to them, you paid top dollar to keep them in good shape, so if they're not you have recourse. Art said he should go with Mrs. Hope to get her things from the vault, just incase the new owners wanted to give her some trouble, they've assured me, that its ok for her to get her things."

Russ got all the Ladies in the van and took them to their Bank (BB&T) to deposit their money, he thought they souldn't be caring around three million four hundred thousand dollars.

Art told Russ, he would meet them at Betsy's old apartment, when they were through at the bank, when they got there, his car was setting in front of it, they all got out of the van, but only Betsy, Russ and Art went into the apartment.

When the new owners came to the door, Art introduced them to Betsy, their names were Nick and Nora House, Nick said "Mr. Moore told us about a secret vault hidden in the appartment and being curious as we are we've looked all over trying to figure out where it could be, but we couldn't find any place we thought it could be!"

Betsy smiled and went to a built in book case removed some books the new owners had place there, she made a fist and with the bottom of it she taped It and it sprang open, then she pulled out a black metal box about the size of a cigar box.

Nora smiled and said "I don't suppose you would show us whats in there"?

Betsy smiled at her, sorry no, but now you have a safe place to keep your valuables.

Betsy thanked them both and said I hope you both have a very happy life here, and thanks for letting me retrieve my box, good bye. As they left the condo, Art told them "good by," Russ asked "how are we going to pay you for you services," Art replied "Bob and I have already taken care of the bill we use your jet service's quite often," Russ replied "that's good to know."

When they all got back into the van, Gail "reminded them that they hadn't eaten lunch and asked were are we going to eat," they seemed to all want Mexican food.

Russ, you ladies will have to tell Sam where to go! They were there with in twenty minutes, and they all eat hardy, Russ was watching, he guessed they were letting go of some of their emotion, most of the things they came to do were done, the only thing left was looking in storage.

When they all got back into the van, Russ picked up the metal box, said this thing is heavy Betsypoo," she smiled at him and said "open it honeypoo!"

He released the latch on the box and opened it, inside were tubes of gold Coins stacked two deep, then she said "they are uncirculated one hundred Dollar gold coins, there's one thousand dollars in each tube face value but There worth more in antque value, and they trade gold on the commodities

Market, so I don't really know what they're worth."

She passed them around for all the girls to see, one of them said "we could all have a gold coin necklaces," Betsy "replied now girls remember that's my future."

CHAPTER 3

Russ told her they need to be in a safe somewhere, she smiled at him and said "they will be just as soon as I find out where I'm going to hang my hat!" he winked at her and said "that will be soon love." they all went back to the hotel, it was about five o'clock, as they went into the lobby, the clerk called "Russ over and told him there was a massage from a Mr. Rice that you should call him as soon as you got back in." He "thanked the clerk and told him he would call him back from his room, they all went to their rooms, as soon as Russ got into his room, he picked up his phone and called Bobby, when Bobby answered his phone, "he told Rusty I have some bad news, and I really hate to tell you over the phone but your Mother is dead."

Russ replied "what?" "she was murdered, the police belive it was done by Chester Potts, he's gone, Rusty you should come home, your house is a crime seen with yellow police tape all around it," Russ replied "Bobby let me call you back in few minutes, the girls have sold their homes, and I don't want to abandon them," and he hang up the phone, and went to fine them, they were all in Betsy's room looking over her gold, he got their attention, and told "them what Bobby told him over the phone, and that he felt like he should fly back to Gastonia this afternoon, what did they want to do," Betsy said "I'm going with you," then all the girls said "they were coming to." he told "them to pack, that he would like to get back before dark, that we will have to stay in the Comfort Suites there, that his house is a crime seen!"

Betsy walked over to him, put her arms around him, and told him she was "sorry that this has happened to him."

Russ enfolded her into his arms kissed her, and said "you have to know that my Mother and father were never close to me, I've always thought that I was an a unplanned pregnancy that my dad made right by marring my Mom."

"So we were never really close, and I always thought they resented me for being born, so as a child I had to overcome both of them, but after I realized It wasn't my fault, it made me smarter just understanding that. And love.

That's just life. In order to grow we have to move on."

Betsy said "I know just how you feel, I had the same problems to." He told her he had to call Bobby back to get us all back in the Comfort Suites in Gastonia," and he called the airport in Waynesville, to get his flight plain back to Gastonia," they told him "his plane was fueled, ready to go." when he got through with the phone, the girls had already checked out, and were in the lobby, waiting on him. when he got to the airport, he generously tiped the driver who had been driving them around town, he diposited them at Russ's plane. it was five thirty as they were flying out of the Waynesville airport, he knew it would take them about an hour to fly back because of the head winds, but they landed in Gastonia in fifty five minutes, when he looked at his watch he was pleased with himself that they made it in that quickly.

Bobby had everything ready for them when they got out of the plane, Bobby told him "the police wanted to see him, as soon as he got back." Russ told the girls "they should go on to the hotel he would join them when he was through talking with the police, and that he would probably have to go Identify his mother's body and I don't think that's something you all need to see." as he started to leave with Bobby, Betsy grabbed his hand, and told him that

"she was going whether he liked or not," he pulled her close "honey Bobby told me that her throat was cut, and I don't want you to see it, she said Mr. Willow, Mrs. Willow is going with you," he smiled and kissed her and said "if you have bad dreams, it wont be my fault."

I know, "let me tell the girls, that we'll see them, as soon as we can," then she got in the car with Bobby and Russ.

When they got to the Gastonia police station, Bobby said "Bo told me to come in the back door, that he would be waiting for us," as they entered the double glass doors, Bo walked up to them and hugged Russ, and told him "he was sorry that this happened to his mother," Russ said Bo, "you know we were never a close family."

Bo said "do you want to go see the body now?" Russ said "we should get it out of the way."

They walked to the police morge, as they entered Betsy shivered and Russ said "honey you ok?" she replied "its just cold in here," when Bo pulled out the body tray, unzipped the cover, his mother's throat was cut from ear to ear he shook his head and said "damn she didn't derserve to die like this!"

Bo said "we know who did it, but lets get out of here, your lady friend is shivering so lets get some coffee, find the Detective's and talk to them, the homicide division, who handled the crime seen, and gathered all the evidence. Will be talking to you, but I want to be there with you!" they walked by an office, with a coffee pot brewing, and Bo servied them a cup, Betsy took a sip and said "this will make the dead walk," she realized what she had said, she turned to Russ, and said "oh I'm sorry, Mr. Willow but that's the worst coffee I've ever tasted."

Bo laughed and said "we need it strong around here, sometime at night we have zombies walking around here, and that stuff brings them back to life!"

Bo chuckled said "sorry rusty, it seam's we're all after you today," Russ said "lets find those detective dude's and get on with it."

Bo showed them into a room with two cops setting at a table, Bo introduced them all to the detective's, "Floyed Wright and Ben Miller," Floyed spoke And said "we are truly sorry for you loss, but we know who killed her, and we are trying our best to find him, we put out APB on him, we did find your mother's car parked at Douglas airport, in Charlotte we impounded it and found the murder weapon, a kitchen bucher knife, from the home, it was put under the driver side, with blood and his finger prints, we ran the prints through the FBI files, but haven't heard from them yet, but we should hear something from them tomorrow." Russ asked "if they looked to see if her bank account was cleaned out?" Ben said "it was, the bank manager said you had put a stop order, on funds from your account, and we think he he found out about it, and he decided it was time to get out of town, so he killed your mother and left town."

CHAPTER 4

Russ told "them about cutting her off from his funds, I had been gone for 2 years, when I finally got back, she didn't acknowledge me at all, and she was in my house, that I had worked my butt off for, and that ticked me off so I cut down her money tree."

Betsy saw he was about to get up set with himself, she touched his arm and said "Mr. Willow, lets just go get something to eat, and get some rest and pick this up tomorrow."

Detective Miller saw it to, "she's right we can do no more, until we hear from the FBI, and I'll call you tomorrow."

Russ got up, shook both their hands and said "if there's anything I can do let me know." they all walked out of the police station quietly, Bo hugged, Russ and said "see you tomorrow." when they all got into Bobby's car Russ asked him if "he would like to go get Something to eat?" he replied, "I should get home, the misses thinks I spend to much time working now!"

Russ said, "maybe you need some help, I promise we'll look at the business, or if you want just do what ever you think is best, I know with a Bank balance like I've got, you've never taken advantage of me, and you could have!"

Bobby looked at him, and said "Rusty Willow you're the only brother I've got and you are my family." when they got to the hotel, and as they were getting out, Russ turned to Bob said "have you talked to Bo, about coming to work for us?" Bob "told him that while he was missing, Bo helped me a lot when I was sick or I needed a break, and he has a working knowledge, of our business, Bob, let me run this by him, then he chuckled, you know the three musketeers back to gather again, don't that sound like fun. Russ smiled, "sounds good to me Bobby!"

He and Betsy walked in to the lobby of the hotel, and the rest of the girls were setting in the lounge drinking soft drinks, when they saw them they all came to him, each one hugged Russ and told him "that they loved him and was sorry for his loss." Russ ask "if they had eaten yet?"

And they hadn't, we were all worried about you!"

He looked at Betsy and asked "what would you like to eat." She looked at the rest of the girl's what will be ladies, and they looked at each other Susan said they use to have some very good BBQ in this area, Russ smiled and said "its been a very long time, since any of us has had any!" he walked to the desk and got direction's to good BBQ place, the guy at the desk said "Backwoods BBQ in north Belmont."

They were there with in twenty five minutes, at the Backwoods BBQ place, they all eat until they were all to full.

Betsy drove them back to the hotel, and on there way back Russ was molested by as many as could get to his tools, and he was enjoying it when Betsy pulled into the parking lot of the hotel, they all got out except Russ he was setting there, when Betsy noticed that he didn't get out, she walked to the van, "now what Mr. Willow, well Mrs. Willow our friends, were playing with Mr. Wiggly, and I'm waiting until he goes down, before I walk into the lobby," she laughed and started to press the matter herself. But Russ stopped her before she could, he said you'll get it in a little while Mrs. Willow."

Russ had a full night with all of his loves, but his resting place was with Betsy, just after he satisfied her, she turned over and he clung to her all night until six o'clock the next morning when she roused him, and said "Mr. Willow would you put that thing where it belongs," and he did when finished he drifted off to sleep until nine o'clock when Betsy roused him with a kiss.

Told him "Bo had called him, and wanted him to come to the station!" he got out of bed a little slow, Betsy chided him to get moving, and he was shaved, showered and dressed in twenty minutes. they all had breakfast in the hotal eggs, sausage, toast and juice and he was ready to roll, he asked "Betsy if she was going?" she told him that "she and girls were going to do laundry in the hotel, she smiled at him and said your shorts need to be washed, kissed him said if you need me give me a call!"

CHAPTER 5

When he got to the police station, Bo took him to a meeting room, and he noticed five guys were in the room, the two detectives Right and Miller Bo introduced him to "agent Hound, agent Clark and agent Stark!" they all shook hands.

Agent Hound said "Mr. Willow after we got the prints on Chester Potts or what ever name he goes by he has a lot aliases, he's been around for about seven years, doing the same thing, fleecing widow's of their money and their lives!

I'm told you have a flight service? yes I do, we would like to employ you to fly us to florida, Mr. Potts is in Florida, we looked at the security tape at Douglas, he thinks he's smart, he bought three tickets, one to Dinver Colorado and one to New York city using different looks, but with facial recognition we know that he went to Miami Florida, the other two flights he was a no show and our agents there are closing in on him as we speak so if you could we would like to get there before he get's wend that we'er close! the Director asked me to get him off the streets, and we thought you would help us!" Russ smiled and said "I would like to see that myself. let me call the airport, I have four jets, but I fly a twin engin prop plane its my favorate mode of travel, so what do you prefer," Wade said you sound like me, so its your choice." he called Betsy and told "her he was flying three FBI agents to Florida!" she said "Mr. Willow you need clean cloths, he chuckled and said I do need somethings for the trip, see you in a bit." then called Bobby to get his plane ready, he was flying three FBI agents to Miami." Bobby replied "you got it chief, but why?" Russ told him "they've found Potts, did you talk to Bo, no, tell him if he don't join us we're kicking him off the three musketeers squad, I think that should get him!" he hung up the phone and told "Wade that he needed somethings to take with him. he turned Bo and told "him he would have to take us all to the airport that he needed to leave the van for the girls." then he took Bo by the sholders, and said "you are working for me and no is not an option!" he left the van at the hotel kissed Mrs. Willow and left for the airport when they arrived Bobby had the engines runing, when he got them all onboard he turned to Bobby pointed to Bo sign him up."

He shut the door and told the agents to make themselves comfortable and told them where the drinks and refreshments were, he turned to Wade pointed for him to set in the copilot seat, he told him it shouldn't take us but an hour or so to get there unless we hit some strong headwinds."

Wade was impressed with Rusty, and felt they could become good friends

Russ told "him about getting lost in the ocean, for two years, on an uncharted Island with eight retired school teachers and we found a paradise, where I think we found the fountain of youth!"

Russ said "but I guess in your line of work, you've heard a lot of stories."

Wade told him that he had been on special assignment for the past few years. the Director called me to take care of Mr. Potts, that he had been a thorn in the FBI side to long, Russ smiled then said "I don't suppose it's because your name's Hound," Wade smiled and said "you got it." They know with my record, I don't give up until there caught or dead. Russ Reached over to shake his hand, and said "Wade Hound-dog your my kind of man."

"I work out of an office in Ashville, I don't suppose you know a man by the name of Gary Pepper? He lived in Stanley before he retired he worked for a bank in Gastonia, BB&T. "Russ asked did he have silver gray hair, tall, you know I do know him, I have an account there to and talked to him quiet often, had a very pleasing personality, very likeable man."

Wade smiled and said "that's him," Russ said "but I haven't seen him in a long time, but I've been away for two years."

We only got back four days ago, and life has been a rollercoaster, sense we got back." Wade said "life is a puzzle, I work with Gary, he lives in place called Stony Knob, just out side of Ashville."

"Well next time you see him tell him Rusty Willow said hello I'm sure he would remember me!" the Miami tower stopped his conversation, and asked for his call letters, then routed him, to the runway he should land on, he taxied up to where he could park, two black station wagons were parked, Russ thought they looked like FBI cars. he helped them to get off his plane, then he asked "Wade, how long do you think we will be here," he told him to "let him check with with these guys!"

Then he would know, he walked over to one of the cars and was talking to one of the men, he turned and motioned for Russ to come over, and told him "to Shut the plane's door." when he walked over, Wade told him "to get in that they had Mr. Potts in custody at the FBI building down town, Wade told him he could go with them that he thought maybe later he could show him something that would be very interesting, to him."

They drove downtown, and into underground parking for the FBI, Wade told Russ as they road up the elevator, "that Potts would be tried for the first Murder in L.A Cal. Then on down the line."

When they got to the fifth floor, they got off, Wade went into an office.

And talked to another FBI agent, he got up and lead the way to a security section of the building, the two FBI agents had to leave their weapons at the desk, and the security officer buzzed them, Russ started to stay out side, but Wade motion him on in, "were going to see Potts," they walked down to the third steel door, and the agent opened the door and inside there was a foyer then a row of bars, and inside sat ole Chester Potts or who ever he was, Wade looked a Russ, and asked "you want to get in, beat the shit out of him," Russ shook his head no, then said Wade "that's not my thing, but I would like to see him fry or hanged, instead of this legal injection crap they have now."

Wade said "at least he's off the streets, and that's what the man up stairs wanted, when Potts got here, he deposited a million an half dollars in a Florida bank, and it's probably your money, but it may be a while before you get it back."

CHAPTER 6

Wade lead them out of the security section, he thanked the guard as they picked up their weapons, when they got to the agent's office "he thanked him and told him the Drictor will be pleased."

Wade looked at Russ and said "the next thing I want you to see, "I don't think your going to belive at first, but it true, and you can't tell anyone

It's a national secret, there would be big problems for you, Wade said "raise you right hand and swear never to reveal what you are about to see!"

Russ thought about it said "Wade I am an honest man, and wouldn't do anyone harm. but maybe you shouldn't tell me, or show me, Wade said "swear to me you will never tell anyone about what I'm about to show you," I Russell Willow

Swear that I will never reveal what you are about to show me to any one!"

Wade smiled and said "now that was easy, the reason I'm doing this is you Told me to say hello to someone, and I'm going to let you do it your self,"

They went into a room, Wade locked the door, and went to a wall where a marker had been placed on it, Wade knocked on a wall, a door opened he told "Russ to come on, he walked into another room, he knew he wasn't In Florida anymore, he grabed Wade's arm and ask "what just happened!"

Wade smiled and said "you just steped out of Florida and into the mountains Of North Carolina."

When he looked around he saw a young man setting at a desk, when the Young man looked he said "hi Wade were we expecting you," Wade asked "Where is you dad?" "He's at the house." Wade introduced "Russ to Gary Pepper Jr." "this is an old friend of your Dads, then he asked if the Chief was here." Gary replied "I think he was here yesterday, but he left early in the evening, said he "had to go fight the fight! whatever that means, I think Dad, was here when he left!"

Russell Willow was in a total melt down, he was looking at Wade and Gary and then around the room, he set down on one of the chair's, Gary Jr. looked at him, then at Wade, then said "its his first time through the door, right!"

Wade walked over, set down on the corner of Gary's desk, "lets give him time to adjust, he's a friend of your Dad's, they are both Koren vets. Russ is a pilot, they knew each other through BB&T.

What made me bring him, he told me to tell you Dad hello, and I swore him to secrecy, and I like the guy."

Wade asked "Russ are you ok," Russ replied "I am, but I'm a pilot and I get from one place to another through the air, I have to adjust to what I just did, then he got up, claped his hands together, it has to be magic, there's no other way!"

Wade got off the desk, then asked "are you ready to say hello to Gary Sr."

Wade lead him down a hall way, then out to a golf cart park.

CHAPTER 7

Russ noticed the mountains and the beauty of where they were, "isn't it beautiful here!" They were in the cart, and down to the house, Russ was very impressed at what he saw, then said to "Wade, Gary has really come up in the world hasn't he," "he has but you couldn't know a nicer guy, Wade pulled the golf cart up to the front door, and they got out, went to the front door rang the doorbell, Sherry opened the door, when she saw who was there Wade "I know you don't ring the bell you always just come in, your family," she hugged his neck, then he introduced Russ to her, "this is Gary Jr. Wife" And this is "Russell Willow an old friend of Gary Sr." "Where is he?" on the back porch, "let me get them for you," she left and came back with them, when Gary saw Russell, he said "Rusty Willow its been a long time," Russ held out his hand, Gary said that won't do and hugged him.

Russ said "it good to see you to," Janice asked are you hungry or thursty she had eaten lunch quiet a few times, with Gary and Russ.

Russ said "I could use something to drink," Wade said "I could to," Janice said "follow me, that she could fix them right up, she asked Sherry if she wanted something to?" She told her "no, she was going up to be with Jr. for a while, I think the schedule was pretty light this after noon!"

Janice lead them to the back balcony, where she and Pep had been setting and enjoying the afternoon, drinking lemonaid, Russ walked over to the rock railing of the porch, and was looking out, at the town of Weaverville he turned and said "now this is what I call living on the top of the world,"

Janice handed him a large glass of lemonaid, he took a long drink and Sighed this is the best I've ever tasted.

Janice said "I wish I could take the credit, but Maria made it for us, she is such a wonderful cook."

Wade was telling Gary how he met Russell Willow, and Russ told me to Tell you when I saw you again. Then I thought he should tell you himself we had done what we needed to do in Florida, and I was coming back today

I'll have to report to the Director, that his mission is complet, and I should do it now, he got up and said "excuse me," looked at Russ and said "I will back shortly we need to get you back to Florida," to get your plane, he went into the house.

Russ sat between Janice and Gary, Gary asked "if he was ok now, with all that mess you ran into in Korea."

"oh yes, but losing all seven of my buddies, me still alive, but I figured out what I did and they apparently didn't know, about the jets we were flying I had a feel for what they were capable of, instincts that I knew kept me alive. but now its all water under the bridge, I've been on an uncharted island with Eight retired school teachers, for two years, they were all from Texas, I found oil seping out of the ground, and with their knowledge of growing up around oil all their lives, we managed to process enough useable fuel to fly us back home.

I've only been back home for five days, my mom didn't acknowledge me at all, the ladies had there home's rented while they were thought dead, at sea

Russ looked at Janice and Gary expressions, then asked am I rambling to much," Janice smiled and Gary said "on an island with eight women for two years, then he said now that's a tale to be told!

And I want to hear all about it from you," Janice said Gary "watch it, or you going to get a knot on your head!"

Russ looked at Gary smiled and shook his head yes!

Russ said "and oh yes, the water was the purest I've ever tasted, and there were trees with fruit that looked like eggplants, and tasted like what ever you wanted to eat at the time. I believe we found the fountain of youth when we landed in the lagoon."

"on the island we were all in out late fifties, when we left it we all looked like we were in our thirties," Gary said "I thought we were the same age, but you do look a lot younger than we do," so where's this island.

Russ smiled, then said "I'm trying to clame the island now. Through my business Lawyer, I'm pretty sure I can find it again."

Gary looked at Janice, and said "should we tell him who stays here as much as he dose in Washington D.C."

Just then Wade came back on the porch, set down, Russ looked from Janice to Gary to Wade, waiting for someone to tell him who stayed here, when Wade saw Russ looking at them, ok what's going on here.

Janice told "Wade about Russ trying to claim an island, and we thought maybe the chief would want to look into it."

Gary said "Russ think's he's found the the fountain of youth and from what we know about Merlin's door, sounds very interesting, what do you think about checking on it."

Wade smiled then said "if that door can do what it can, I think anything is possible!"

Wade smiled we could run it by him and see, he then looked at Russ and said "you young man need to be thinking about going back to Florida your plane is there, and the way you talk about it, I know you want to get it back home!

Russ got up and said "your right about that, that lady and I have been good friends for a very long time, she was my first airplane, and now we have four Lear jets that crisscross these United States and the World, but she was my first love."

He look at Janice and Gary and said "before I leave can I hug both of you

Its Been and honer and a priviledge to have seen you again after so long a time, but nobody has told me who the Chief is yet?"

Wade looked at Janice and Gary and said "maybe we should wait until we talk to him about Russ's Island. is that ok with you Russell? Russ smiled then said "that will have to be ok,

I think to much of you to question anything say."

Russ hugged them both, he and Wade left the house and back up to the barn and back into the building, and back into the room with the door

Sherry and Gary Jr. were eating, he stopped eating came over to the door with Wade and Russ, he asked "Russ if he had a nice visit with Mom and Dad," Russ smile and shook his hand, and said "I did, I love them both and Its not always easy for me to say that!"

Gary Jr. put his hand on the door, Wade put his hand on Gary arm then he opened the door, Wade said thanks "son, just leave it open for a bit I have to get Russ out of the building and transportation to the airport!"

CHAPTER 8

As Russ was riding back to the Miami airport, he was thinking did all of this really happen, then he realized it was all true that there were things in this old world that didn't make a lot of sense, and this was one of them. but he did really like seeing the Pepper's again, and hoped he would see them again.

The FBI agent pulled up beside his plane, he got out and "thanked him for the ride."

And he was in the air headed home, a thousand thoughts were runing through his mind, then he thought of Betsy, and that brought him back to what really mattered in this life.

As he approached the Gastonia airport, he gave his call numbers, and Bobby Replied, its all clear come on in, when he taxied up to his hanger, he noticed All the ladies standing waiting on him to get out of the plane.

And he wondered what they were doing here, when he opened the door, the Guys from the shad were chocking his wheels.

When he stepped to the tarmac, all the girls came up to him with huggs and kisses, Betsy told him that "they had released his mother body, for burial that Bobby and Bo, had already made arrangments for the burial, tomorrow If that's alright with you."

He looked at her, kissed her again, and said "you know I'd already forgot about her, the FBI has old Chester Potts, behind bars, with seven counts of murder. I think he will fry for his deeds."

Bo and Bobby walked over and ask, "if Betsy told him about tomorrow, he told them she had," he hugged each of them, and asked and pointed to Bo "he's on the payroll right, Bobby with a big grin, I told him "he was off our team if he refused, he retired this morning."

"They didn't want him to go and offered some attractive incentives, but l offered more."

Russ said "the boy is worth it, now I've got to get some food, he pointed At Betsy and between her leg as soon as I can," he winked at them, and said "See you tomorrow. (and Thanks for everything, I love you guys)"

Betsy had the van and the girls loaded, he had told her "he was hungry for Food and her."

As they left the airport, Betsy asked "where they wanted to eat?" Russ said lets "go to the Cracker Barrel, and they all thought it was a good idea." they ate, and went to the hotel, Russ told them that he was tired, then he asked "if they were going to the funeral tomorrow, that if they didn't want to go it was ok with him."

From what he heard, they would be there, he kissed them all goodnight, he "whispered to Betsy, that she would be comeing to bed with him," she smiled said "Try stop Mr. Willow," he got a shower, before Betsy snuck in to the room, she said "those women, were watching me like a hawk.

I think they knew I was going screw you brains out," Russ chuckled pulled her to him, that's just what I think I need." they did make love for hours, they would sleep, wake up and make love again, until they were exhausted, until two in the morning.

He was awake by seven thirty, showered and shaved, when he came out of the shower, Betsy. Was still naked, when he saw the beautiful pinkness of all he had enjoyed last night, his body responded, then remembered he had to put his mother in the ground today, and that thought brought his body back to the reality of what he had to do.

He got dressed, set on the side of the bed, and kissed her, when her eyes opened she smiled and said "boy were you hungry last night," he smiled and said "I was, when I came out of the shower this morning, I was about to pursue some more of you charms, Mrs. Willow." then I remembered what I had to do today, and "if you don't want to go through it with me, I'll understand!"

She smiled, then said "Mr. Willow, where ever you go I will go also, he kissed her again, and said "now that's my kind of woman."

Betsy was up bathed and ready to go.

CHAPTER 9

To his mothers funeral, Russ didn't expect to many people to be there, his mother was not a personable person but he thought he should be the one to put her in the ground, but he was not looking forward to doing it, but he knew he should do it, there was nobody else, no brothers or sisters and no grandparents. all his life he had been lonesome for love and affection, but from his parents none ever came!

Bobby Rice, Bo Arrow and Rusty Willow where there for each other all their lives.

Most all his teachers, made him aware, education was essential for his life ahead. All the girls came into the room, ready to go to the funeral, Rusty was not aware that the funeral home, would provide transportation for them when they started for the van, a nicely dress young man came up to them,

Mr. Willow this way, and escorted them to two black lemos.

On the way to the grave yard Russ was aware, that there was conversation going own around him, and would respond when asked something, but for some reason he was reliving his whole life with the assholes that he had to endure his whole life.

But he had made it and quite well, when they arrived at the grave side they all got out, walked over to where he was supose to set, and was surprised to see all the guys from the Work Shed, and the charter service he went to each one of them and thank them.

But when he got to Bobby and Bo he hugged them and then he lost it, not physically and he didn't think emotionally, but tears came like a waterfall but finally the funeral was over they led him away, with a roll of paper towels damn near used up, Bob, Bo, Betsy got him in Bo's car, and took him To a bar, and tried to get him drunk as a skunk, but he didn't get drunk he got sick as a dog.

They finally decided to take him to the Hospital, and there they pumped his stomach after that they gave him something that made him happy, and very sleepy.

After Bob and Bo knew he was alright, they left him in bed at the Motel in Betsy's capable hands.

And he was asleep for a good fifteen hours, when she woke him up, she Started kissing him, until he responded to her, he smiled at her and said "now that was one hell of a ride."

She told him "the police had released his house, would he like to go check It out, he said well it is mine, but I'm not sure we would, want to live there

What do you think?"

Betsy replied lets go look it over, mabe we will want to keep it, Bo called And said "they had cleaned out the bed room you mother was in so lets get You ready, the girls want to see it."

Russ was showered and shaved in twenty minutes, and was ready to roll When thay all got out side Betsy lead them to a brand new Cadillac four door escalade, Russ asked "when did this happen?"

She told "him while you were sleeping, I got the girls to go get it, it was Their choice and with my approval, she said I can afforded it."

When they got to his house, the yard had been well groomed, his mothers corvette was setting in the garage clean and shinny.

They all got out walked to the door, Betsy opened it and they all walked in every room they went into had been cleaned, and the room his mother died in had been cleaned out. all the ladies gathered in the den, set down, and were talking "to each other and they all decided they wanted to live here."

That is if Russ says "it ok with him, Russ came in from the garage, inspecting the corvette.

When he walked into the room, they all looked at him, Betsy smiled, and told him that all the girls liked his house, he sat down with them, then said "that he had always enjoyed living here, this place was something he was proud of, because he had worked hard to get it. and it was a place he could raise a family of my own, but it just never happened.

But as I look at each one of you, you are the only family I've got, he smiled,

I love each one of you, a fellow could not ask for any thing more.

There are three bed rooms, that's what we have in the hotel, we have two and a half bath room, we may have to make the half into a full bathroom, the bedroom my mother was in had a full bath, and that one I claim, now its your job to furnish it for me, please, I don't want pretty things in it but something, that would appeal to a man, for all your convinces, of coarse so when do we want to move in, I think it ready for us except my bedroom and the half bath, the decision is yours!"

Betsy put her arm around his neck, said "I'm ready to do it today!" he said "well love living in a community, were going to have to at least appear that I'm not sleeping with all of you, which I'm going to be doing, until you stop me from doing it Mrs. Willow."

Betsy smiled and said "life was more simple on the island wasn't it love."

He took her into his arms and said "I hope we will be able get back soon,"

CHAPTER 10

It took the girls a week and a half to put the house in order, for all of us to live there comfortable, they had added another bedroom with a bath made the half bathroom into a full bath, and built a seven foot privacy fence in the backyard, with a large bed with a roof and sliding glass and screen door's which Russ and all the ladies had already tried out, they all thought it was a lot like the cave, they had lived in for two years, Russ missed seeing them all naked laying together, and how beautiful their bodies were and his body responded to each one of them all night long, when he woke up at ten o'clock the next morning, he was alone, he wondered where Mrs. Willow was, as he was trying to get out of their bed, he noticed that a few things were sore, then he couldn't remember how many times he was with each one of them.

He went into the house to take a shower, Betsy was drinking coffee, she smiled and said "you wore us out last night, I think the girls all went back to bed, "I wore you out! I'm the one who can hardly move," went over to her, he was still naked, she started playing in his tool shed, it responded she laughed, he picked her up and put her on the table and had her again, then picked her up, took her into the shower with him.

When they got out of the shower, the phone rang, Betsy picked it up, and handed to Russ, she said "its Bobby, he wants to talk to you," hi Bob, you should come down here, I just had a very interesting conversation with Jeff Hobart, he wants you to contact him as soon as you can!"

"we'll see you in about fifteen minutes, ok!"

Russ said "Babe lets go to the shed, Bobby sounded excited about a phone call he got," "sound's like fun to me but you have to buy me an icecream before we get back."

"you got it babe," walked out of the house, Betsy started for the Cadillac.

But Russ stopped her, and said "let's take the corvette," they got in Betsy smiled "this is our car right, you got it lady," Russ had forgotten how power—ful a car it was.

He soon realized, if he didn't watch it he would be getting a speeding ticket. they were at the work shed in no time, he parked in front, Bo came out to in see him in his new ride.

Bo smiled then said "now that car is you Rusty," Russ smiled and said "if I drove this thing to much I'd have more tickets than I could pay for," Betsy said "I think he cute behind the wheel, he's my kind of man."

They got out of the car, walked in the office, "hi bobby who called, that got you Mr. Cool excited," "well Russ the guy is Jeff Hobart, who has over the years made you a rich man, he's been using our shop services to fix most of his jets, at least the ones his shop can't fix, he didn't tell me why he wanted to talk to you, he knew I ran the place, but that I didn't own it, he gave me this number to call," Russ said "well we don't want to keep one of our best customers waiting." he called the number, when someone answered, "he told him who he was and that Mr. Hobart left this number to call him, he said "hold on a minute let me see if I can locate him, he came back to the phone, I'm is his son Larry, Dad's down at the cottage by the river, let me patch you through to him," Russ said "thanks Larry," when the phone was pick up it was a women she said hi this is Mary, Mr. Hobart please, she told him to pick up he said "this is Jeff," Russ said "Mr. Hobart this is Russell Willow you wanted to talk to me." Jeff asked "where he was," "I'm calling from the work Shed."

Jeff told him he and his wife are setting on the deck down by the river, eating ice cream would you like to join us," "sure that was one of my wife request, that I had to get her ice cream before we went back home."

You will go through our gate, I'll call and tell them that your coming Russ "we'll see you in twenty minutes!"

Betsy heard that, "well, well Mrs. Willow is having ice cream, Bo said "your going down to the Adams place, now that is big time, he's one of the richest men in this county."

"well I'll see you when we talk to Mr. Hobart," he and Betsy were there in fifteen minutes at the gates of Adam's mannor Russ pulled up and told the guards at the gate, that Mr. Hobart said "he would call to let us in, the guard asked if he was Mr. Willow and asked for I. D. Russ showed him his drivers license, he told him, he would have to go up to the house, but that someone at the house would take us down to the cottage." when they both saw the house, Betsy said these folk have made it, an old English Tudor home, they pulled up at the front door, a young man came up in a John Deer cart, and told them to get in, that he would take them down to his father.

Russ said "you must be the person I talked when I called," yes it was me, Mom and Dad love it down by the river, and I love it there to, I grew up there.

He circled around to the back of the house, then down a paved driveway, to Betsy it was the most beautiful landscaping she had ever seen, and told "Larry that it was," he pulled up beside the cottage, took them up to where Mr. and Mrs. Hobart were relaxing eating icecream, they both got up and introduced, themselves, "Mary and Jeff Hobart," Russ introduced him self then he introduced Betsy as his lady."

When Russ said "that," it sent a thrill up and down her spine, she shivered but she didn't think they saw it.

Russ walked over to her, put his arm around her, asked "you cold babe?"

She smiled at Mary and said "I want some of that ice cream." Mary said honey let me get you a bowl she put her a good portion in her bowl of Lucille Best Ice Cream!

Russ got some and they set down, and were enjoying each other and the companionship, Russ asked "Jeff if he knew Gary Pepper he lives just out of Ashville a place called Stony Knob."

Jeff thought for a minute, "smiled "I do know him, he eather works for the President, or is friends with him I've met him once, he was with the President, he seemed like a very likeable person."

Russ said "the reason I asked, I knew him when he worked for BB&T in Gastonia he was a good friend when I needed a friend."

"his home look's a lot like yours, I believe the President visits him often," Jeff said I think "he's in the armament business, I remember something about a bullet they invented, it helped the military and the police." if I am correct he's a very rich man, and he could be donating a good bit of money to the President's party, I've given my share, I'm a fan of the President."

Jeff said "the reason I've invited you here, I want to buy your company, as you know we do a lot of business with the Work Shed, and we've got a charter service that has no rivals, and we've noticed that your company is gaining ground, with four Jets in the air!"

Russ replied, "you do know that I've been out of the country, for two years not voluntarily of coarse, I took a group of teachers to Barbados, and coming home we encountered one hell'va storm that I thought would kill us all, but as fate would have it, we found an island that was uncharted, and we lived there for two years, we've only been back for two weeks!"

Jeff "I read about it in the paper! and saw it on the news," Russ said "Bobby Rice an old friend of mine since childhood, ran the business for me, and he added the other two Jets! So any—thing we do, I'll have to run it by him, he's the brains behind the business of coarse it's my business, I worked my ball's off to get it started so what kind of offer are we talking about. Jeff smiled and said "how about Fifty

Million dollars," Russ smiled then said "that's a nice chunk of change." how long is the offer on the table, I will have to talk to Bob and Bo another member we just added to our staff, he's another one of my friends we grew up together, I got him onboard, because Bobby was working to hard, and when I got back, I was surprised that I still had a company, Bobby, Bo Are my child hood friends, they keep me sane! when I needed it most!"

Jeff said "you don't have to give me an answer now, the offer isn't going away, we want you company, talk it over with your crew, and get back with me when you've decided."

Russ smiled and said "Jeff you are my kind of man, lets walk down to rock I'm want to see it, I can hear the water runing, and it sound so soothing, I bet its hard to stay away from it."

Jeff put his hand on Russ's sholder and said "I've lived on this old rock my whole life," when they got down to the end of it looking at the river below, Russ asked "can I set down and dangle my feet off the edge," Jeff smiled and said "of coarse. this place is really my home, I've skinny diped off of this old rock just about all of my life, Mary and I have had a lot of fun here."

As Jeff, and Russ sat with their feet dangling off the rock, Mary and Betsy came down and sat with them, when Betsy first set down, she put her arm around Russ and asked "is this the same hight as our water fall," Russ said "I think the water fall is a little higher, but isn't it peaceful here, it reminds me of the peacefulness of the island." they set for a good fifteen minutes, just enjoying the sound of the water runing past, until Russ thought and said "well honey I think we've worn out our welcome," Jeff said "like heck you have seeing it through your eyes has made it even more fresher than it has in a long time.

Its heaven on earth." Russ said "that it is," got up and helped Betsy get up waited until Jeff and Mary got up, they all walked back to the cottage, Betsy told Mary that this is just a perfect place, Mary said "thanks, we love it to"

Jeff laughed and said "I wonder if Larry left us a ride down here." He looked and there was, Jeff asked "Mary if she was ready to go up, she laughed and said if we don't Martha will give us a fit."

As Russ and Betsy were getting into the car, Russ told "Jeff he would let him something in a few days."

Said their good nights, as they were driving down the mountain, Russ asked Betsy if she heard what Jeff offered him for his business, she said "no honey Mary and I were eating that delicious icecream, she was telling me who made it and it was someone in her faimly.

Russ said "honey he offerd me Fifty Million, smackers," Betsy laught and said "that's a lot of smackers."

She said "you know what I wanted to do, at the river, I wanted to get up, and take off my clothes and jump into the river, wasn't that a perfect spot,"

Russ said "Jeff told him, that's what they did skinny dip there all the time, and make love."

Betsy smiled and told "him that's what I shivered about I was wishing you could have me there."

Russ drove back to the shack, to see if Bob and Bo where there, and they were, they were talking to each other, when Russ and Betsy walked into the office, they both turned, and Bo said "ok give it up what, did Mr. Hobart want? Russ said "he wants to buy our Company," Bob stood up and said "what did! you tell him?" I told him "I would have to discuss it with you guys, and the employees of this company. Now I started this outfit, on a shoestring, with the help of a lot people. Bob you most of all, with your business acumen, and with the work ethics that, demanded from every one who worked for me, and Bobby that includes you!"

Betsy "Russell Willow tell them what he's going to pay for this company,"

Bob said "thank you Betsy, Bo said spit it out Rusty!

Russ sat down then said "this is more fun seeing the look's on your faces it's like the first time, we all had Patsy Eller, for breakfast, dinner and supper.

Bob and Bo started laughting, Bo said it's got to be good, remember how good she was, I think we followed her around for months, hoping we could get a repeat performance.

Betsy said "watch it children there is a lady present." Russ said "sorry love but that was a time before we knew what we carried between our legs could give us so much pleasure."

Then Russ asked "did you guys ever get her again," Bobby said one time for me, Bo said "once for me, to I think Bobby had just had her, because I met Bobby a little while later he had a big grin on his face, but he never told me why," Russ with a big smile held up ten fingers, I think I loved her but old Arnold found out, beat the poop out of me, told me never to tough her again, you remember me coming to you all beat up, and we went and found him and we all three beat the poop out of him, but she must have loved old Arnold, because she wouldn't have anything to do with me after that and believe me I tried.

Betsy said "boy's that's enough! Jeff Hobart, offered Russ, Fifty Million dollars, for his company, now the thing is are you going to take it." Bo said that much money, wow, Bobby said I think we should take it, holy cow, fifty big ones.

Russ said "I had a lousy family, but two of the best friends, that ever lived so lets get the whole gang together tomorrow, and talk about what we're going to do.

Bo said I just arrived, so what's this going to mean to me, Rusty smiled and said you have got it made, Bo Arrow, I don't think Bobby or I could let you down.

Russ said "Bobby get the whole company together tomorrow, at ten o'clock to see what they have to say about it all!" but as for me I think we should except Mr. Hobarts offer, we will all have enough money to do what ever we want.

Betsy smiled and said "we could go back to the island, and build ourselves a really nice home, process the oil to run a generator for electricity and for fuel for the plane, then we could go anywhere we wanted."

Russ said "honey that sounds like a good plain to me," Bobby and Bo got up to leave, as they were leaving Bobby was singing you're a rich girl, and you've been gone to long, but it really doesn't matter any way, you can rely on the old man's money. He said "a little (Hall & Oats) for the boss."

Russ got up and said "I think they liked the idea of us getting rich."

Bobby came back into the office, "there was so much excitement I forgot to give you this, Betsy it's the report the lab sent back on the samples you sent to them, I didn't open it because I don't think I would understand anyway." he hugged them both, and out the door whistling to him self.

CHAPTER 11

Betsy said "this should be interesting," she opened the envelope and pulled out two sheets of charts showing, what was in the samples they analyzed with a cover letter saying you may have found something like the fountain of youth—please contact us as soon as you can! and gave an address. Betsy handed it to Russ to looked it over, he said "honey this could be dangerous if this gets into the wrong hands, and puts the word out that we have found the fountain of youth."

"I think some people would kill to get what we know! and to know where its at." then!

Russ said "don't worry love, I think I know who to contact about this!"

When they got back home, the girls had fixed a fine supper, they all eat,

Russ told them "he had to make a phone call." he got Wade's card out and called him, when he answered, Russ told him who he was, he said "hi Russ"

"I got a lab report on the samples we took from the island, let me read what they said, you may have found something like the fountain of youth. contact us as soon as possible! should I send it to you or Gary," "Russ send it to me with an overnight courier, use the address on my card, but use a black marker to put att: Wade from Russ," "Wade I'll send out to night, and thanks," he called the UPS service, they picked it up with in twenty minutes

Betsy wanted to know "what I was doing, I told her he was sending it to an FBI guy I know." he whispered to her to come to bed with him, when she could, he kissed all girls and said "he was tired and was going to bed." when he lay down he started thinking about the meeting he was having tomorrow, he tought it would go well, that he would try to take care of them all. then another thought crossed his mind, and it was about sweet little ole Patsy Eller his first love she was two years older than they were, but she made it heaven for a while for all three of them. When Betsy got in bed he already had a tent, when she saw it, she laughed, Mr. Willow, "what brought that on," he chuckled and said "you remember us talking about a young girl by the name of Patsy Eller, I hadn't thought about her in years, until it floated up tonight, while I was talking to Bob, and Bo when I came to bed, I was thinking about the meeting we're having tomorrow!

Before I knew it, turned to sweet Patsy, I guess she being my first time and that is why this has developed, but now that it has, I'm expecting Mrs. Willow to help me out with it, and she did for a good portion of the night."

The next morning after shaving, showering and breakfast he told all the girls about Jeff Hobart buying his company, and to be thinking about, if they wanted to go back to the island.

Betsy told them about "building us all a home on top of the mountain, with electricity, anyway be thinking about, I know I'm going, if Russell Willow goes I'm going."

Russ asked Betsy to go with him to the meeting. and by the way, when are you going to marry me, she looked at him, and said "I think I'm already married to Mr. Willow," he smiled I think so to, "but its not official, so before I become a very rich man you better grab me while you can,"

"she smiled I'll think about."

When they got to the Work Shead, Bobby and Bo had the whole crew there, Russ got on bench to address them, "he told them he thought they already "knew why they were here and asked what they thought about him selling the company?"

Albert one of his oldest employes, said "Russ for that kind of money you would foolish not to sell," Ralph joined in, and said "the same."

Russ told them "that Jeff Hobart is a good man, I think he will pay you more than old skin flint Bobby Rice, he looked at Bob and said you know I'm kidding." then he told them that he didn't have all the particulars on just what Mr.

Hobart want's or what plans he has for this company, but I do know he has paid us a lot of money over the years, and that he's is impressed with the work you guys do in the Work Shed!

As am I, we built a solid little company, that is now worth, a tidy sum today Mr. Hobart will get the four jets, the travel services, but what I think he really wants is you talents as A-1 first class Airplane Mechanical Doctors with work ethics that are second to none!

And I'm sorry to have been gone for two year's, I think you all know that it wasn't my fault, and Bobby took care of all of you in my absent, but I am ready to move on with my life, and selling the company will give me that opportunity! I will set each one of you up with a retirement program, that I think you will like, and approach Mr. Hobart to match it, I understand he's one of the richest men in this country. I hope you understand, where I'm coming from, now let me talk to Mr. Hobart to see what he has in mind.

Albert and Ralph you guys aren't going anywhere, what would I do with out you guys to help me keep my baby flying.

CHAPTER 12

Now let me get out of here and find out just what Mr. Hobart has in mind for us all." As he and Betsy were getting into the Vet. Russ ask "was I clear enough did I do that ok!" Betsy smiled "sure love I saw a lot of smiles when you told them about the retirement plan's!" they drove down to Adamsville and found the Adam's Bank, went inside a redheaded lady came up to them, she asked if he was Mr. Willow, and took them up to the second floor, Jeff was setting at a desk, with Mary setting **b**eside him, they both got up and shook hands, with Russ and Betsy and said "they both enjoyed there company yesterday evening, and said we should do it again."

Jeff ask "Russ if he had made up his mind about selling his company," Russ replied that "he was, but do you want the physical property or just the people that work for me." the "Work Shed, the people that work in it, I've built a new facility at

Adamsville air port and the people you have are the best, the planes and the travel sevices will be merged into what we already have, Russ said "there's a couple old heads that I won't let you have and the prop plane is not for sale, but if you want I'll get them to ease my crew into your's and if you want to use them from time to time its ok, and I'm giving all my employes a retirement package of one hundred thousand each, and was thinking if you do the same, that would show them you were interested in their well being and they are good people, and the Gastonia facility, you will take out all the equipment, Jeff said "we'll only take out what we don't have, but I think we have in this new facility with all the latest equipment."

Jeff looked at Mary and asked "if she had all that down on paper," well Russ think we have all we need, I'll fax this over to the office, and the company Lawyers can work up the sales contract, that you can sign, and you will be a wealthy man, that is if that's what you want."

Russ replied I'm already wealthy, in a lot of respects, but this will allow us to go back to our island," he took Betsy's hand. kissed it and said "well babe, I think were on our way."

Russ said, oh yes "did you agree on the one hundred thousand for my employees!" Mary said "that will be in the contract," Russ said "that's good just wanted them to have something when they retire, Jeff replied, "Russ that money will grow over time, and who know's what it will be when they retire.

Russ smiled and said "that's even better, Bobby always handles my cash flow and he's gifted that way, he and Bo Arrow are my oldest friends, we grew up to gather," and I plan to take care of them, I haven't figured how much they will get, but I owe them a lot, we helped raise each other, when you come from a uncaring family, you learn early, how to survive but I'm not sure you would understand where I'm coming from."

Jeff smiled, then said "I was raised by my Brother, he was more like a father, and a cook who was more like a mother, who still think I'm a child, she chides me, often, but I love her more every day."

Russ smiled, then said "I would have thought you would have everything, that life had to offer, coming from your background.

Jeff said "a lot of what you say is true, but I grew up here in Adamsville, and I was always Sam Adam's grandson, but the textile business wasn't something that I wanted to do for the rest of my life, I always tought that my grandfather Adams wanted me to be a part of it, so after he died, my father and brother took over the business, and I ran off and joined the army for a three year hitch, and during that time my brother and both my parents were killed in a plane crash, but what brought me back was, and he looked at Mary, that lovely lady over there, I met her on a cold rainy night, soaked to to the skin, standing in phone booth, in the middle of nowhere, her father had pick her up at school, they came by and saw my plight and took me in, when I first saw her, and those beautiful blue eyes, I was a total goner, and I've been following her around ever since." the phone rang Mary picked it up, she turned and looked Jeff, and said "guess who looking for you, its time to eat, Jeff look at Russ and Betsy want "to go with us, to lunch it'll be good, my mom only cook's the best."

Betsy said "yes I'm hungry, Russ smiled and said of coarse," Jeff said "the paper work will be done," by the time we get through eating lunch, and you will get to meet our family!"

Jeff picked up the phone and called the house, and talked to Millie, tell "Marty to come pick us up, and tell Martha she is having company, yes two more."

Jeff, Mary. Betsy and Russ walked out of the Bank, got into the lemo, Jeff talked to Marty, and introduced Russ and Betsy to him, Marty replied that he was pleased to meet them, he droped them off in front of the house.

Betsy told Mary that she was excited to get to see her house, Mary said we love it here, Jeff's grandfather built it, in the eighteen hundreds but it hasn't lost its charm over the years." they all washed up, Mary lead them into the dinning room, and started introducing them to the family, this is my mother, June my dad Bob Smith,

Lucille, my other mother, this is my other dad John Fox, and by the way the icecream we had last night, was made by Lucille Fox, which is Lucelle Best ice cream," Betsy "Lucille's Best, I've eaten a ton of her icecream, it's best on the market today, she looked at Lucille and said "thank you for making it for us all," Lucille said "no thank you for buying it."

CHAPTER 13

Just then Millie came into room with platters full of food, Jeff asked where's Martha, Millie smiled, she's got Dr. Wilcox in the kitchen stuffing food in him, he's grumbling and she's fussing at him, they're fun to watch and you know how she is Jeff." they all started helping them self's, and eating, when Larry came from the kitchen, "Grand maw, caught me coming in and made me eat, she and Doc, are still fussing at each other, when he saw Russ and Betsy, he said hi to them, then looked a his Mother and asked "do you think those two will ever get married," Mary told him at there age she didn't think so," Larry replied "we all know they love each other."

Jeff said "well son the old saying, you don't buy a milk cow, if you can get all the milk you want free!" Mary said "watch it, Mr. Hobart those are young ear's your talking to and I want Grandbabys runing around in this house."

Larry said "mom I'm not a child, and that day is getting closer than you think." Mary said who? Bee, yes and she coming over after lunch and were going swimming down in the river, and I don't want to be disturbed by any one from this family," he looked at June, Bob, Lucille and John said "huh I think I might just have to go skinny dipping right after lunch!" Larry said "well Dad can I use the cottage, I don't want her to have to look at the old people naked, John smiled and said "us old people don't look half bad in the buff you young whipper snapper."

Larry started chuckling, "I'm sorry grand paw, my intent was to get some alone time with some one very special to me."

Mary said "son I'll keep the old fogies away, I promise they will not bother you and your lady friend."

Betsy chuckled and said "skinny dipping sounds like fun to me!" Russ said "honey didn't you hear, Larry just said some alone time," oh love I was just kidding," she winked a Larry.

Millie came into the room, and said "Jeff the bank just called, the paper's you were waiting on are there.

Jeff said "I guess we can go now and make you a rich man Russell Willow."

Mary asked "Jeff if she was needed anymore," "no honey all I have to do is get Russ's John Hancock on the documents and give him his money."

Jeff, Russ and Betsy got up to leave, Mary said "I promise to have you back and we can go skinny dipping for as long as you like, unless your shy about being naked," shy, "did Jeff not tell you about us being stranded on an Island Russ/eight ex-school teachers, "after the first few day we were ether naked or half naked, and Mr. Willow had a ball." Mary said "sounds like fun to me, when you come next time, you have to tell me all about it, that sounds like quiet an adventure." when they got back to the Bank, they set down in Jeff's office, Russ signed all the documents one of the tellers from down stairs witness the signing and notarized them, but Jeff didn't let her know how much money was involved in the transaction. then Jeff asked "how do you want to do this, you want me to transfer money to you accont, Jeff said "let me put it to you this way, I can hand you fifty mil. in one thousand dollar bills, or transfer to your bank that amount, but if you put that much money in your account, the tax people will grab thirty to fourty per cent of it, or you could leave twenty five million here, and I could transfer twenty five million to your account at BB&T. or you could rent one or two of my large safty beposit box's and put the whole amount in thousand dollar bills there, and no one would know that you had that kind of money at all, Russ said "you could give me fifty mil. dollars right now?" Yes of coarse I'd have to get it from the vault down stairs Jeff said "this is a private bank, my grandfather set it up so he wouldn't to have the approval of the government. and now it's all mine, so what's you choice," Russ said "could I see what a million dollars look's like in thousand dollar bills," Jeff said "sure there's 2 hundred thousand in a money band, if you and Betsy will go down stairs and get some refreshments I know your not hungry, but theirs is all kinds of soft drinks down there, the peach soda is really tasty, I think I'm addicted to the darn things."

When you get back I'll have what you asked for, and if you would bring me one of those peach soda's please!"

Russ and Betsy were gone for about ten minutes, jeff got the money from his and Mary's play room in the closet. when Russ and Betsy steped off the elevator, Jeff had his money setting on a cart beside his desk, Betsy smiled and handed the drink to Jeff, he thanked her and took a big drink, and said "Russ this is your fifty million dollars, in a lump sum, then he picked up five stacks of thousand dollar bill's this is a million dollars."

CHAPTER 14

R uss sat there for a minute, then said "that's mind bogging, to see fifty million dollars setting in front of me like that," Jeff said "its you choice, but like I said "in an FDIC bank, any deposit of ten thousand and over is reported to the I.R.A. for tax information, that will come back and bit your butt, so to speak, now I'm not trying tell you what to do, I'm just giving you options," then he pulled out a tape recorder, and a nickle palted automatic, these are just things to keep you from bitting me in the butt. so what is you poision, sorry just a figure of speech.

Betsy said "Honey Jeff is giving us a golden opportunity, and I think we should take it."

Russ smiled and said "the deal is "do, done and did" he got up and shook Jeff's hand and said "thank you!"

Jeff said "we like to keep these thousand dollar bill in our bank, so you can get ten one hundred dollar bills for each of them, the thousands you can spend but there usually passed from bank to bank."

Jeff said "let me go get some boxes, so we can get to the vault, I trust all my employee's, but what they don't know thay can't accidentally repeat to another party."

I'll be back with three box's, mean while if you two will count the money, and Russ the money for the twenty five employees, that's two million and five hundred thousand, to deduct from your stack.

When Jeff got back Russ and Betsy had counted the money and it was all there they had counted out the two million/ five hundred thousand, Russ asked if he could open four more lock boxes, Jeff said "sure we have the space," they loaded up the box's and Jeff gave him a receipt for the money in the employees names and Jeff put his hundred thousand with Russ's, so he felt good about that, he had gotten lock box's for Bobby and for Bo with two million each, two for Albert and Ralph with one million each for them. when they were through, he had fourty one million dollars in the Adam's, bank and if Bobby and Bo wanted more they would get it.

Jeff "thanked them," and shook hand's and told Betsy we would get together soon.

As they drove away from the Adams bank, Betsy said "do you feel rich yet!"

Russ "no I don't think so, I've never felt poor, but sense I met you and your friends on the island, I have truly been blessed with so much!"

Russ said "lets go by the Shed, I want to give Bobby and Bo some of my good fortune."

When they pulled in front of the shed, they walked into the office Bo and Bobby were setting and talking about the good old day, when they were kids they both smiled when Betsy and Russ came in, Bob said "the Hobart crew has already been here, they taged two machines in the shed to be moved

Russ asked where's Albert and Ralph, "you know there working, those guy's work like beavers, if a jobs to be done they don't let any grass grow under their feet, Russ smiled I guess you know those guy's help make the Work Shed what it is.

Betsy handed Russ two Adam's bank pouches, he sat down and handed one to Bobby and one to Bo, and he waited until they opened them, Bo had his key out first, then asked what's this, Russ smiled and said "look inside there's a deposit slip," Bobby had it out first, his eye's got big, then he said two million dollars, Bo pulled his out then, "we got the same."

Russ said "that's tax free money, the keys are to a lock box in the Adam's bank in Adamsville, and there's two million in one thousand dollar bill's which they will exchange for hundred dollar bill's.

Now if you want, you can take it out, but if you put it in another bank, you will have to put less than ten thousand dollars, because an FDIC bank will have to report it to the IRS, and I'm like Jeff Hobart, you don't want to stir up that kind of (dodo) are we clear?" they both started laughting, Bobby said "I think we get your drift chief."

Russ smiled at them, "there could be more if you needed it, because blood is thicker than water," Bo said "we not blood kin, Russ looked at Bobby, did you forgot to, "heck no, still got the scar, and I bet Bo still got his remember he cut mine, and I thought he was trying to cut my thumb into so I fixed him up," Bo looked at his thumb and said "sorry guy's its was a long time ago, and if I remember correctly it was Russ's knife, I didn't know it was that sharp."

Russ looked at them both and held up his thumb, "brothers all way's,' they put them to gather, Bo said "brothers all ways," Bobby said we are the three musketeers."

Betsy said please, "you knuckle heads," you're not children anymore," Russ smiled replied in our hearts we are."

Russ now "lets go make two more good men happy, so they all walked from the office into the Work Shed, when they entered they could hear the guy's banging and talking, when they saw Russ and his gang coming toward them they stopped working, Albert looked a Ralph and said "I'll bet that turkey going to fire us." when Russ heard that he replied, this turkey going to show his apparition for all the loyalty, and hard work that you have given over the years.

He handed Ralph his bank pouch first and then one to Albert they both unzipped them Ralph pulled out the key and slip then he smiled and said "this is for me!"

Albert when he saw the amount he said "hot dog!" He turned to Ralph and said "this is one nice payday," they both grabbed Russ and gave him a bear hug.

Then Russ gave them the same speech he gave Bobby and Bo, and asked if they understood, Ralph said yes, "you don't look a gift horse in the mouth!"

Russ said "even though you both got a million a piece, you still work for me, and we still own this property, you still have to come to work, I might be persuaded to let you have a nice long vacation."

"Bobby and Bo will have to figure out, what we want to do with the place!"

Bobby said "we could easly rent the hangers," Russ said "that sounds good to me."

Russ said "you all might want to think about a nice long vacation you all deserve it!"

Russ hugged all the guy's and told them, "you're the best!" he pulled Betsy to his side and said "let's go babe, you and I got things to do when they got to the vett. Russ said "I'm taking you to South Carolina and we're getting hitched," how romantic she said, "then that's a yes." before she could think about it, they got married in South Caroling before a justic of the piece, and finding a motel, and so began their wedded bliss, Russ had a very good night, he thought mabe Betsy had one to because she required him to please her once more, before getting out of bed. when they were showered and out of the motel, he took her to jewelry store and wanted to give her a three and quarter carat diamond, but she refused it she thought it was beautiful, but not practical, she said "Mr. Willlow on the island we won't need it, so she got her self a nice carved wedding band and one for him to, he told her "what ever you want you get love." when they got back to his house, Gail told "him a man called four times yesterday, she thought his name was Wade H something, that you should call him when you got back!" the girls all wanted to know where they were all night, Betsy smiled and showed them her ring, they just looked at her strangely until Betsy pulled a bag from her purse, and handed each one a ring just like hers, Russ looked at her, "when did you do that, when you peed, she kissed him and said Mr. Willow when we all go back to the island, we will all want to screw your brains out."

CHAPTER 15

When Russ heard that smiled and called Wade, when he answered his phone told him "that the President was very interested in there discovery!" and wanted to talk to you about it, and he would like for you to meet him at Gary Pepper's place in the mountains. its sounds ok to me, but Wade I just sold my business and was going to fiy back to the island.

Wade said "the people that reviewed your lab reports will try to contact you and Russ some of these people are not to be messed with and if they come after you, well lets just say, to get what they want they would kill you." I would feel better in here! in this compound with us! "wait a Wade!

How in the hell did they get a look, at what I sent you, "Russ it's a long story, that I can't explain over the phone, where are you now at my house in Gastonia N.C., are the ladies there with you now? Yes Wade said, "gather them all together in one of your bedrooms, give me the location," Russ said "why?" Wade said "because your all in danger, Russ said "we can't let anything happen to them," so give me your location, street location and house number, Russ gave him all that he asked, went and called Betsy into his bedroom, and told her that this is going to sound strange but get all the girl's into my bedroom now, she looked at him strangely, honey believe me, this has to be done now, she got all the ladies into his bedroom just as a door opened from the wall and Wade and Gary stepped out, Wade held up his hand, "I know you will have a lot of questions, but they will have to wait for just a little while." as he and Gary lead them through the door, it only took a moment to get them into the compound, Wade tried to explain what just happened but he could see it would take a while to understand, Janice was at the desk when she saw Russ, with all the women. she smiled at him, came over and hugged his neck, Russ introduced "Betsy as his wife, then introduced the girls Susan, Gena, Lola, Gill, Gail, Sheila, and Martha Janice told "them we have a place for you to stay here in the compound it will be comfrotable we often have troops here, and have two squads in house today they are on the other side of the compound, and Russ has been here before so let him explain, what happened to you, Wade your staying aren't you, yes but the ladies would be more comfortable, down in the apartment, Janice said "it would be to cramped for all of them, and they can eat in the mess hall not to worry."

Janice told "Gary there one more coming thourgh, so you will have to show them, where to bunk down," he lead them through a maze until they were at a section of squad room's with five room's, the bed's were like dorm rooms neat and comfortable, with two chairs and two lockers, Gary said "you can decide, who go's where, Russ will tell you about the door, this is a secret facility, so when you leave here, you will sign wavers before you can leave that you will not discuss this facility.

Russ "try to explane to you friends, what just happened to them, he smiled if you can," patted him on the back.

We will talk to you in about thirtfy minutes, "we've got one more coming through."

Gary, said "I'll see you in thirty minutes and left them," they all looked at Russ, "I really don't know I've only been through it twice before, myself that was Wade idea, "I told him to say hello to Gary Pepper, when we were in Florida, he told me to say hello my self, and I stepped through a door from there, then I was in the mountains of North Carolina. then he looked a Betsy "they have a home a lot like Jeff and Mary in Adamsville, it is beautiful, I also went back to Florida through the door I had to pick up my plane to fly it back, so I really don't know anything other than its magic!

The reason we are here is because I sent Wade the report on the samples we sent to the lab at home, and they wanted us to contact them immediately saying it was urgent, it implied that it contained something like the fountain of youth.

And I thought Wade should hear about it, but somehow the report got into the wrong hands, and he though we were in danger, and we are here and that's all I know."

Russ pushed a botton on an intercom, and Gary said "hi Russ what do you need," "I just wanted to take the ladies out side so they could see that they are really in the mountains," "well don't be surprised if you see Marine's patrolling the grounds, and stay close so I can find you, and we'll take you down to the house, OK."

Russ said "sure, I wanted Betsy to see your home," "see you in a bit," Russ said "just how do I get out of here," Gary chuckled, then said "follow the hall and it will lead you to an exit door, don't run out or act suspicious, those Marine's have loaded wepons, OK."

Russ said "I under stand nice and peacefully," Gary said "you got it," when they got out side, all the girls were ohing and ahing at how beautiful the mountains were, Betsy looking at the house, said "isn't that the most beautiful place you ever seen," Russ said "its as nice as the Hobart place, don't you think."

Betsy looked at Russ, and said "can I have a place this nice," he said honey on the island, I believe you could have one even nicer."

Betsy smiled, and said "you know I belive we could have, and I would like one setting on top above the waterfall so I can jump into the lake below like we used to do, naked as a jay bird," all the girls replied "that sound's like fun and we did have a lot of fun."

Russ smiled, a lot of fun, they started walking around what looked like a barn on the exterior, but look solid as rock, when they got to the other side they saw a Marine walking the primerter of the rock wall, he looked and smiled at the girl's and they waved at him, he salute them and a big smile, he looked like a teenager, but a well built, young man, Betsy said (the few, the proud, the Marines) Russ said sounds good to me, that's what made this country, "who we are."

They heard a loud speaker, calling for Russ to "come around to where the carts were," so they all headed for where the carts were park. when they got there Janice and Gary were waiting for them, to go to the house, Gary asked Russ "if he could drive one," Russ chuckled, and said "if I can fly a plane surely I could drive one of these things." they got them all down to the house, in two carts, Betsy was admiring the Pepper's house as they got closer to it, as she got out of the cart, she commented on how beautiful it was up close, she said "they must be very rich people."

Russ said "honey, your one of the richest people I know."

Janice took them all into the house, and ask "if they would a like a tour and after we could get some of Maria's french apple pie, does that sound like a winner," they all chimed in "you bet."

When Gary heard that Janice was giving a tour, he looked at Russ, "lets you and I go out on the porch and have a cold one," so the girls went one way and the guy's headed for the deck, they sat down and poped the top of on a Dr. Pepper.

Gary said "so Russ how are thing's going?" well Gary I'm at your house because our friend, Wade, said "somebody get hold of a report, about the samples we took from the island, we were stranded on for two years, and the lab came up with, the samples contained something like the fountain of youth."

Gary said "that's what's different about you Russ, you look younger, the same as when I first met you," Russ "that's been a few years!" "when you just got out of the military, how old were you at that time?" Russ replied just twenty two years old, Gary shook his head, that just can't be, then he laught, "listen to me, I inhered a door, from my uncle, that take's you any—where you want to go."

Gary said "so maybe you did find the fountain of youth."

Russ said "so that's where that door came form, and that's more of a mystery, than anything I can think of."

Gary smiled then said "you know that only Janice, myself, Gary Jr. and Sabrina my daughter, are the only people that can get it to work."

Gary told him, "that in the will his uncle left, said that the owner of Merlin door can use it, they found it in an antique shop in London they had it for two years, before they found out what it could do, my Aunt bought it because she loved the carving on it, my Aunt and Uncle could read latin, and that they saw Merlin name on it, and thought it was valuable."

Then he told "Russ, about the CIA breaking into the house and stealing it one night not long after we first use it, we brought the grandkids up to the house that night. and the next day they stole it, but Wade and is crew, stole it back, that's the for reason for all the security."

That could be the reason, the CIA intercepted the report, you sent to Wade, that's the reason he came and got you all, with a report like that, they would do anything to find out where the samples came from, "and the safest way was to bring you all here, because this place is safer than Fort Knox the President come's here all the time."

Russ said "the President of the United States come's here," Gary Smiled and said "Andrew probably told Wade to keep you out of harms way, and that's why your are here."

Just then all the ladies came out of the house onto the deck, Betsy said "so this is where you guy's came to, she turned to Gary and told him that he had a beautiful home," he thanked her, and said "we love it here to." all the girls were looking out at the town of Weaverville, and exclaiming how beautiful it was out here."

Gary asked Janice had she noticed how young looking Russ was? she said "you know I thought he look the same as when we first met him."

"do you remember him telling us that he had been on a deserted island for two year's."

Yes and no "I was just gald to see him after all these year's," "well he and these beautiful young ladies, were drinking from the fountain of youth."

"What she exclaimed," she laughed and said "I just thought Russ, was trying to corner the market on beautiful young girls."

Well that's explains why you all are here, with Wade, "I'll bet the CIA has something to do with all of this, (bingo) you got it!"

Gary said, "now where is it, because we need it now!" Janice chuckled and replied your right about that, she looked at Russ and said "when can we go"

Russ said "I know the latitude and longitude, and with your door we could go anytime, just say the word.

CHAPTER 16

Janice smiled at Gary and said "love I need it now!

Gary looked at his watch we should eat something, it almost two o'clock!

Betsy looked at Russ, "we could eat on the island," Russ looked at the Peppers and said "we could go now, there something there good to eat!"

Gary got up looked a his wife and asked "are you ready love!" and they all went back up to the compound, then walked into the door room

Gary said "we should call Wade and see if he want's to go, is that all right with you Russ?" sure!" it took Wade five minutes to get there, Gary told "Russ to put his hand on my arm, and think where we are going!"

And Gary opened the door, and they all stepped out close to the waterfall

Gary, Janice and Wade stopped and were just looking, around Russ said "ok you guys, lets go get something to eat, Russ said "the girls can stay here" the three of us will go get the food," you will be surprised at what we get then he turned and told "Betsy to show Janice where we lived."

Russ lead the way up the steps to the top of the water fall, and crawled into the cave, he told them he had to get something to carry the food in when they got inside Gary and Wade thought the moss covering felt like thick carpet, they looked at the raised area in the middle, and they both laid down on it, Russ chuckled and said "that were we all sleep," Wade said "it's comfortable enough," then he asked was it fun sleeping with eight women

Russ smiled, then said "we thought we would be here for the rest of our lives, and yes I made love to all of them, we useally sleep naked and yes they all had need's and of coarse I had need for them all."

Russ found what he was looking for, a net he used to carry the purple fruit with. as they headed down the other side of the mountain, he showed them where the oil was coming out of the ground, and the still they used to cook their fuel, Wade asked "how long did it take with this primitive method?"

Russ smiled and said "a heck of a long time, I think it took a good seven month's after we got the hang of doing it."

"it all started after I learned what was in the pool, I begain using it for torch's in the cave at night. and around the lake, when it was hot inside, then I learned that all the girls were from Texas, and I asked, "if they new anything about refining oil? and we finally figured out how to do it."

"when we were making it I thought it was a lot like making moon shine." just as he had finished telling them about the oil, they stepped in to the grove of trees with a purple fruit hanging from the branches.

Gary said "that's not suppose to be, egg plants don't grow on tree's."

Russ laughed and said "that's what I thought when I first saw them, but that's not the surprising thing about them."

Russ got them to hold the net, and he pulled off fifteen, he pulled out a pocket knif. then cut one into peaces, and handed a piece to Gary one to Wade, told "them to take a bite, and they did." when he saw the look's on their face's, then he asked, what are you eating

Wade smiled then said some of the damn best chocolate cake I've ever eaten." Gary started laughting, "you know what, I love pizza, and this is the best, then they looked at each other, Wade said "how can this be" Gary said "beat's me."

Russ let them think about it, then said "it's what you mind want's. to eat the old adage mind over matter, must be true," Wade and Gary quickly grabbed the rest of what was in Russ hand, and consumed it quickly.

Russ said "you guy's were hungry, I'm glad I got my hand out of the way before you decided you wanted it to." they both laughed, Gary said "lets get one to Janice, I want to see how she react's." so they headed back, Russ had the fruits on his back, when they came up and went by the mouth of the cave they could hear women giggling an as they passed by the water fall out came Janice naked as a jay bird plunging into the lake below.

when Gary saw her, he said "I can't belive she would do anything like that, but I did like what I saw."

Wade said I'm going to razz her about it, Gary said "no you want!" the older we get the less she want my company in bed, and I still want her.

And two more came out through the water fall, and one of them was Betsy

Russ said "how did you like that boy's, she rock's my boat, and often!"

Wade said look in the pool, there all naked, and I like the look's of that!

Gary said "Wade cover your eyes, seeing all that will make you go blind.

He smiled and said "can I look until I need glasses."

Russ and Gary both laughed at that, Gary, said "OK Wade that might be acceptable."

As soon as Janice saw them coming she quickly got out of the lake and quickly put her cloths on.

When Gary saw how quickly she got out, he hollered at her it's OK honey I enjoyed what I saw.

She hollered right back, you shouldn't have been looking, Gary Pepper and you ether Wade Hound.

Wade said "I had my eye's closed I swear."

Gary, he did honey I put my hand over his eye's. I did'n want him to see how beautiful you look naked. The other girl's didn't seem to mind them looking, it was OK, when they gathered around them, to get some thing to eat, they did put there panties and top's back on. the girls took the egg plant's over to the lake, and rinsed them off, Russ said "these thing's don't have any spray on them, Gill said "my mom always rinsed her fruits off before eating."

He said Ok love, what ever you want, Russ cut them into four pieces. then said "Janice has to eat first, so he handed a piece to her and told to eat," she looked at Gary, he smiled and said "it's OK honey, I've already eaten some." she took a bit and a look of amazement came to her face, she said "Maria's French apple pie."

How can this be, Wade said "my exact words, Gary shook his head in in agreement." the other girls were all eating something different, and nobody stopped eating until they had consumed four more of the fruits. then Gary, Janice and Wade were discussing how that could be.

Russ told them the only way it could work, is you mind wanted it to taste like something you wanted to eat.

Russ said "these things sustained us for two year's." we didn't go looking for anything else to eat, we were full all the time.

Janice asked, can we take some to Andrew? Russ said "I don't see why why not!"

Gary said "so this fruit and the water, is what the lab say's is the fountain of youth?

Russ said "we gave them sample's of the water and the fruit, and Wade you read the report."

Wade replied he did, then said "what we need to do is take sample's to a top Government lab, and let them test them, and not tell them were they came from."

Gary said "I'll have to go get some jug's to put the water in and some large zip lock bags for the eggplant looking things."

Then he asked Wade, if he could think of anything else we would need?

Wade said "we should ask Russ, if all of this would be OK to do."

Russ said "it would be fine with him, the only thing, I'm not telling you where we are, because of the boondogle with the other lab test's."

Wade smiled and said "that's understandable, but you know it wasn't my fault, the guys at the CIA are all way's checking on me, it seam's that I have a very good record for finding and stirring up the pot, I try to keep them off my back, but as you've seen they are good at what they do!"

Russ said "I wasn't blaming you Wade, but there is probably some one in your group that's leaking information, gathered by you, so if I were you I'd find out who it is."

Wade replied, I only go through the Director office, and I don't see how, anyone there could or would pass anything on to the CIA, Russ said "well right now it seam's you got problem's, and maybe there is some house cleaning in order, for the Hound dog dept. of the FBI."

Gary asked Janice where would I find, gallon jug's and large zip lock bag's she said "honey there lot's of full jug's in the storage locker, you will have empty the water out of the jug's, and ask the cook in the mess hall, for the large zip lock bag's. then she said "I think I should go with you, you could get the Water jug's

I'll fetch the zip lock bag's." they walked over to where they had come out of the rock wall Gary reached into the rock wall and opened the door, and before stepping into it, he turned to Wade then said "it shouldn't take more than twenty minutes." they were gone, Russ asked Wade "if he would like to go skinny dipping?"

Wade smiled and said "Russ if I go skinny dipping with all the beautiful women, Mr. Happy might stand up, I would be embarrassed, if they saw it,"

Russ smiled then said "Wade if that happen's float on your back and see if one of these beautiful ladies will take the bait, you never know, it could happen, because they are a horny lot!"

He smiled, you think, out of his cloths, and into the water, it wasn't long and he was floating, Lola found it appealing, and had him dancing in the water, until he shouted (holy moly). and in a few minutes the Pepper's came out, with four Jug's a hand full of large zip lock bag's. they took four jugs of water from the water fall, four of purple fruit's Russ asked "if they missed something?"

Wade, Gary and Janice looked at him, Janice asked "just what am I missing"

Russ asked "have you been pestered, by mosquito's, fly's, any kind bug's."

Gary said "going down to get the fruit's, I was expecting to be bite by some kind of bug's but nothing!

Russ said "we were here for two years, no bird's, we saw no fish nothing

My thought's were that this Island, has never been inhabited by and living thing other than the tree's plant's, and of course us, we tried not to pollute even our body waste melted into the ground, I built one facility, of coarse I built it Military stile and it's still there." he pointed to where it was, he ask them "if they had ever heard of any thing like this.

Gary said "this would be a scientist dream discovery."

Russ smiled, "I don't want it for science, I want it for my home, as soon as I can claim it, for all of us, this is truly a paradise."

Russ showed them the sign the girl's made for him, "I've staked my claim on this place already." WILLOW ISLAND and with the oil reserves "I can put generators, for all the electricity needs we would have, if there's enough we could sell it!"

Wade smiled and said, "let's get these sample's back so we can get them tested," he looked at Gary and said "we know somebody that could get this island claimed for you, by just using a pen."

Russ smiled and said "the President!" Gary looked at the other two, and said "how did you know," Russ said "I just figured it out, with all the security you have, the door, and you mentioned the Chief several time's the first time I came here, and it was an easy assumption to make, Russ smiled then said "I've all ready signed, a none discloser on the door?

So you have no worries from me."

CHAPTER 17

Wade said "we should go, and get these samples, to a good lab, I know it **h**as already rejuvenated me," Gary said how? Wade, he replied I had a very nice encounter with that beautiful red head over there!" Janice said "you did what with that red head?"

Wade smiled then said "a gentleman never tell's, she smiled at him then said "Wade you deserve all the fun you can get, you always work to hard it's time you started enjoying your life, more power to you!"

Russ told the girl's it was time to leave, then they all started grumbling can't we stay, Russ smiled then said "I want to stay to, but, I not ready to divulge where we are, not under these circumstances, with threat's of bodily harm to us, we will come back, soon."

They all walked back into the compound, Wade pulled Russ aside and asked if he could pursue Lola, that he hadn't felt like this in a very long time, and if she would want to be with him, he would marry her."

Russ smiled them said "Wade you will have to talk to her, she is a lovely girl and I would think, she deserves to have a good man like you, so you go for it, all she can say is no."

Wade smiled and said "maybe I could come back to this island again, I know I'm going to drink the water, and eat some more of the purple fruit

I want to feel like I felt with her in the lake."

Gary and Janice, told them all that they were tired, and would see them tonight for supper, that they were all invited."

Wade told them "he needed to call the Director, to find out where to send the sample's of what they brought back from the island."

He then talked to Lola, when they parted they were both smiling.

Betsy asked "if Wade said anything about Lola,"

Russ told "her about what Wade had asked him, he wanted to know if he could persue Lola, I told him of coarse."

Russ and Betsy started for the barraks, a long with the other girl's.

When they got back to their quarters, they paired off in two's Russ and Betsy went into one room, he asked Betsy if she was tired, she smiled at him, and said "no but I think when we are through, we will be, she took off his cloth,s then her's, then she turned him everyway but loose, when they were snuggling after the glow of having sex, and Betsy had drifted off to sleep.

He had just about to drift off him self, when he thought, about the money he had left in the trunk of the Corvette, after leaving the Adam's bank.

He gently pulled away from his love, kissed her on her ear, and told her he had to call Bobby, he put back on his cloths, to go serch for a phone, he found one just out side of their room, picked up the recever but there was no dial tone, he went in search, of one of the military people, but could find no one, he decided to take a cart down to the house. when he got there, he rang the door bell and Maria open the door, he asked where Mr. Pepper was? She said she thought they were on the deck in their quarters, Russ asked if it would be OK to go back, she said "I would think so Mr. Russ," "hank you Maria," he went to the deck, and saw the Pepper's having a personal conversaton on a shase lounge, he stopped, smiled quietly turned around and went to find Maria. when in went into the kitchen, the smell's of food cooking, made his stomach turn over it smelled so good. when he saw Maria she asked "if he had found them? he told her they were sleeping and he didn't want to disturb them," he said "all I need is to find a phone he could call out on," she showed him one in the kitchen, he asked "if he had to dial nine or something to get out," she said "no that the whole compound had secure phone line's."

He called Bobby at the Shead, and Bo answered, he asked "where are you Rusty?" Bobby is out looking for you, Russ you know how Bob is always's trying to take care of us," Russ chuckled, well he's got our butt's out of trouble quiet a few time's over the year's."

Bo said "I know that Russ," Russ said "you tell him I'm OK, I'm in the Mountain's of North Carolina, with all the girl's."

I want "you to do me a favor, we left the house in a bit of a hurry, I'll try to explane when I see you guy's!

Go by the house, I left the key's to the Corvette, on the kitchen table, open the trunk, there's a box take it out and put it some place safe it contains a good bit of money in hundred dollar bill's, if you guy's need any feel free to take it. At the moment I don't know when we'll be back, I'll check in with you guy's as often as I can," Bo said "Rusty you know I've got a lot questions to ask," Russ replied "Bo I know, just tell Bobby we're all safe,"

Bo said "you know Bobby, will have the FBI looking for you," Russ replied "tell him not to bother that's who I'm with, and that's all I can say, keep an eye on things and watch your back's, use you instints as a cop," he hung the phone up.

When Russ said "that and hung up the phone," Bo thought what the heck is going on, and when Bobby came into the office, he told him about calling,"

Bobby said "what the heck is he into now" Bo replied, "he told us to watch our back's so something is going on," he pulled out his sholder holster with 45 automatic in it, and gave Bobby one to.

Bo said "Rusty told us to go to his house, and retrieve a box in the trunk of the Corvette."

They went over to Rusty's house and when they got there, there was a black wagon setting in the drive way with Fed. plate's on it.

Bo pulled his car up to the bumper, to keep it from moving, he and Bobby got out of the car, and slowely approached the house, the garage door was open they looked around in the garage the Vett. didn't look like it had been tampered with so they slowly approached the door to the kitchen it was open, they heard men talking, Bo pulled his weapon, whispered to Bob to do the same, pointed to the safety off, opened the screen door, eased into the kitchen a few draw's were standing open, the voices sounded like they were in one of the bedroom's, they eased up the hall, until they were at the room the voices were coming from, Bo steppen into the room with his wepon up them Bobby did the same, Bo asked them "what they were doing and it startled them, one of them started for his wepon, Bo clicked the hamer on his gun, and said I wouldn't, if I were you, and in police fashion shoved them into the wall, and told Bobby to "shoot their ass's, if they try anything. he shoved their feet apart, and pulled out their wepon's and tossed them on the bed, then pulled their ID from their inside pocket's. handed them to Bobby, and asked him to tell him who these a-holes are, Bobby said "their ID's say their FBI," Bo said "I know better than that." then he told "Bobby to find some lager electrical tie's so we can restrain them "until we can find out just who they are what there doing here in Rusty's house."

Bobby returned shortly, with the tie's handed them to Bo, he made the two men put there hand's behind their back's, just as he started to do it, the two men tried to do some fancy ju-do move's, but Bo was much faster than they were he smacked them both down on the floor, when their head's hit it they were out cold, Bobby said "way to go my brother Bo."

Bobby laced their hand's and feet with the tie's, Bo sat them up against the wall, pulled out his cell phone, and "called the Gastonia police dept. and asked them to patch him in with the FBI office in Charlotte."

When they answered the phone, he asked "to talk to the agent in charge," they patch him into agent hatfield, Bo told "him who he was, and asked if he had any agents by the name's of Lester Flint and Leroy Mc'Coy then he said "I don't know those name's personally, but let me run it through the system's to see if they show up any where else in the U. S. personal files in a few second's he came back."

They not our's, then he said "let me run them through another group, he came back," "they work for the CIA, and you said "they have FBI I. D.'s

Bo told him he was looking at them, we should be their in thirty minutes to pick them up."

Bo "told him to notify agent Wade Hound, if he could do now!" "sure thing, Wade moves around pretty fast." they left the dud's on the floor in the bed room unconscious, Bobby got some rope and tied them up more, Bo laughed and told him they're not going anywhere, then he gathered the wepon's off the bed. and they went back into the kitchen, and started looking for something to eat Bobby said "this police work has made me hungry," they found a jar of roasted peanuts, and diet mountain dew's, and they were munching away when they heard the guy's in the bedroom, "threating to lock them up and throw away the key's."

Bo sat and listen to them for a while, then he said, "that's enough," he found some duck tape, tore off two pieces, gave Bobby one, they went into the bed room, one of them said "who the hell do you think you are," Bo chuckled

"I could be your worst nightmare," he put the tape over their mouth's "if I hear anymore crap out of you, there is a dull kitchen knife in the kitchen, and if I have to I'll cut your little pecker's off, do you understand, they looked at each other and shook their head's.

As Bo shut the bedroom, he told "them there is someone coming for you in just a little while, so remember the dull knife!"

Bo and Bobby went back into the kitchen, and continued munching on the nut's for about fifteen minutes.

CHAPTER 18

It was supper time at the Pepper house, and they were all there, Wade, Lola, Russ, Betsy, Gena, Martha, Gill, Gail, Susan, and Shela, as they ate, Wade asked "Janice where the kid's were, she told him that "they had taken a few day's off the to visit Sherry's family, and Brent's folk's, they said they needed to get a way for a couple of day, they went out this morning around eight, said "to pick them up in two day's."

Maria walked into the room, and told "Mr. Wade there was a phone call for him," he was out of the room less than five minutes. when he came back, he said "you will have to excuse me we have something important to do, Russ let's go, Gary if you would please." they all headed up to the compound, driving up in the cart, Gary told Russ thank you," "what did I do, that you need to thank me," "well for one, thing Maria said you came back and found us asleep, and we both know that the chase was rocking pretty good, because I was knock, knock, knocking on haven door that's one, and what ever is in that water on the island my wife is responding beautifuly to it really, really well, so if I could I would like to put a hundred gallon tank fairly close to the door, and pump it full of that water," Russ said "it sound's like a good plan," Wade said "I've talk to Lola about getting married," she said "it was fine with her if you and Betsy approved."

And as they pulled into cart park, Wade told "Russ about two guy's being caught in your house claming to be FBI agent's, two guy's whose name's Bobby Rice and Bo Arrow, had them restraind and was waiting for them to be pickup, so that's what you and I are going to do. if we can get to the bottom of this problem, you guy's can go on about your business. when they got into the compound, Wade said "let me get some body restraint's for our brother FBI fake's, and they went to the door, Russ said "if I know my brothers's there in the kitchen eating my vittles."

Gary put his hand on the door, and told Russ to put his hand on his and to think where he wanted to go!. when he opened the door it was into a bedroom of Russ's house, no one was in it, Russ told them "to be quiet," he wanted to surprise his Brothers they sneaked down the hall way, when he looked around the corner into the kitchen, Bo and Bobby had their fourty five's trainded on them, Bobby said

Rusty you son of a gun, we could have killed you, Bo said he heard somebody whispering and sneaking down the hallway and we thought it was the butt holes we have stashed in the bedroom on the left side of the hallway."

"I think we would have shot them, because we've had all, were going to take from them."

Russ introduced them to Wade and Gary, Wade said "I remember Bobby from the first time we met, Bo I don't think was there, he and Gary shook hand's with both of them."

Wade asked what are you eating, Bobby said all I could find was these rosted peanut's, Rusty said I hadn't even opened them, and there all gone

Bo look at him and said "you wouldn't deny a brother a little food would you, Russ hugged them both and said you know you can have anything I've got! Bo said "we know Rusty, I was just pulling your leg." Gary said "what have you got in the fridge, we didn't get to eat, before we came," Russ said "set down boy's and I will feed you a meal you wont soon forget, he had brought one of the purple thingies, with him, he retrieved four plates's from the cabinets, washed the eggplant, dried it off, cut it into five pieces of an inch and a half thick, Bobby and Bo looked at him as if he had gone mad,"

Wade said "they not had any of this, before have they?" Russ said "nope and there in for a surprise."

Bobby said "to Bo are you going to eat that mess," Bo said "look at that fine fellow he wouldn't give us this if it wasn't the best," Gary and Wade had started on their third piece, Gary said "just stick into your mouth and eat when they did such a look came over their face's Russ, Gary and Wade were looking at them and the look on their faces, finally Wade asked what are you eating, Bobby said "I'm eating the best fillet's stakes I ever had, and he consumed it very quickly," and said "can I have some more please?

Russ cut him another piece, another strange look came to his face.

Bo stuffed the last piece into his mouth and laughed that was the best pizza I've ever eaten, can I please have some more, Russ chuckled and cut him another piece and he started eating it, he said "French apple pie, wow is it good, Bobby said "you should try the strawberry short cake its very, very good to."

Wade and Gary had gotton the last piece, Bobby said you guy are pig's eating the last piece like that. then they all started laughting, at them self's, Bo asked what was that, Rusty Willow, Russ said "what ever your mind want's is what you taste, is the best way I know how to discribe it."

Wade told Russ to look at the clock, they had been there for three hour's.

Russ said "we had better get a move on the ladies are going to be worried about us."

Wade walked into the room and looked at the two men, "yes I know these two they are CIA and from them we will find out how they are getting all the information from the FBI, he reached into his coat pocket, pulled out a metal tube unscrewed the top and pulled out a syringe full of something, Wade said "this will knock them out, but make them mobile, can walk but can't talk, if you guy's will hold them down, I'll put it in their upper leg, this is powerful stuff it shouldn't take but a few seconds." he turned to Bo and Bobby and said "now you guy's will have to leave, before we do, we came here in a mannor that you can't know about, and it might just blow your mind's if you knew about it."

Russ hearded them out, and told them to get the box out of the trunk of the Corvette, and hopefully we can get back to a normal life soon.

Bo and Bobby were concerned for him, he assured them that he was safe but I can't tell you how I got here, because of a piece paper that said if I tell anyone about this mode of transportation, I could be put into a federal prison."

And you guy's would lose a good man, so wait out side until I turn the light off, when I do that besure to take the money from the Corvette, if you need any of it feel free to take it.

Russ went back into the house, Gary opened the door, and Wade pushed the zombie's through it.

When Bobby and Bo saw the light go out they went into the house looking for their buddy, neather was Wade or Gary.

Bo scratching his head and looking at Bobby, said "that Rusty has got himself tied up into some really weird (do do) and what do we do about it,"

Bobby said "Rusty is no dummy he can take care of himself, if he need's us he will hollar for us."

Bo said "now let's go raid the fridge, they took some stuff from it," then Bobby saw the new add on the back of the house, he motion for Bo to follow him, they went out on the back deck, walked over to it Bo pulled back the sliding glass door, and said "would you look at this I'll bet it's a boody shack," Bobby said "there's eight women following him around, can you think of all the fun that rascal has had and is having."

CHAPTER 19

When Wade, Gary and Russ walked into the compound, Wade turned over his prisnor's to two Marine's that were waiting for them.

Gary, Russ and Wade rode back down to the house, on the way Wade told "Russ this could be the answer to who and why this all happened to you!"

Russ said "if you only answer to the Director, there's got to be a leak, in his office, or someone working for the CIA," Wade said "I think the Director will have to clean his own house, I will contact him, when we get down to the house." when they went into the house, all the girls were playing card's, they seemed to be having a good time.

Wade left them to check with the Director of the FBI, Russ and Gary sat down and the girl's delt them into the game.

Maria came in and asked if they wanted something to eat? Gary told her "we had something at Russ's place, but if she had some French Apple pie I'm sure we could handle some of that," Wade came back into the room, and chuckled then said "the

Director was highly ticked off, said "he would get to the bottom of this mess, even if he had to resign, that he was getting sick, of that bunch of hoodlum's over at Langley."

Russ said "that is the right attitude, to take, when somebody's screwing with the best law enforcement agency in this country."

Wade said "your right about that, I think some head's will roll, this time."

Maria came back with some French apple pie, Gary, Wade and Russ inhaled all she brought.

When Janice saw the way those guy's were eating her French apple pie. When Maria came to see, if the guy's wanted more, Janice told her, "she thought they had enough of her pie."

Betsy looked at Russ, and he knew she was ready to go, Russ got up rubbing his stomach, Mrs. Pepper I very much liked your pie, I'm sorry to have eaten so much of it, but these other two gentleman, Mr. Hound and Mr. Pepper got more of it than I did, I really had to hustle to get just a little bit of it."

That brought a chuckle from the other's, Gary said "you were going after it so fast, I was just trying to keep up your pace, Wade smiled and said "I've seen pig's that would envy the way you two were eating Janice's pie."

Wade got up from the table, then said "I'm tired, I think I'll turn in, then all the girl's were getting up and telling Janice, that they had a very good after noon."

And as they left Janice hugged them all, then told Russ and Wade they could have all the pie they wanted.

Wade told Janice and Gary he would help Russ get all the ladies up to the bunker, and they were gone. when they got to the bunker, Wade pulled Russ aside, and told him he was inviting Lola to spend the night with him, Russ told him it was fine with him that she deserved, to have a fine man like him, Wade and Lolo got back into cart and were gone. when they got back into their quarter's, Betsy said "she needed to shower so she took off her cloth's, the more she took off the more his (thing's) wanted to take a shower with her, when they became wet, he started washing her back, her front part's, then he coaxed her to bind over for him and she did willingly, she smiled and said "have at it Mr. Willow, and Mr. Willow did just that, it was so delicious he did it twice. while in the process, of his second round, the other girl's came into shower they were watching him as he finished."

Susan said "I'm next, Gena me to, Martha after you, and pointed at Gena, Gill I'm getting in on this to, Gail me to, Sheila well I'll take it when I can get it." when he and Betsy were finished, he held her close for a little while, then he saw all those beautiful bottom's waiting for him, he became inspired again, Betsy smiled and said, "go to tiger, and he did, when Sheila had enough of him, his member was so engorged, he had to take a cold shower to get it back to it's normal state. when he finally got back to his room, Betsy was already sleeping, he crawled into bed with her, pulled her close, and drifted off to sleep, when he finally woke up, he was again by him self, he wondered where she was, but he guessed she thought he needed the rest.

Russ go up shaved and put his clothes on for the day, then went looking for Betsy, all the room's were empty, he thought that was strange, went outside and ran into a young Marine, coming into the compound, Russ asked "if he had seen the girl's this morning," well sir, "I saw two cart's full pretty girl's going to the house just a few minutes ago," he "thanked him." there were no more cart's, so he started walking down to the house when he got there, there were a group of people in front of the house. then he realized what was going on, someone was getting married, he saw a preacher, talking to a couple in front of him, then he saw who they were, it was Wade and Lola, he thought that was fast, but what he knew of Wade, he was sure he would be a good husband for Lola. when he got closer, he saw Betsy, she turned and saw him, and eased out of the crowed and came to him, she asked if he had eaten, he replied no, I was worried about you, then she said "Mr. Willow you are a grown man, and I know you can take care of your self."

Russ said "what happen to shiring our load, side by side."

Betsy oh honey, after last night, we all thought you needed the rest, come on I'll take you into the house, and get Maria to give you something to eat, they walked into the house, went into the kitchen, Betsy asked if she still had some breakfast, Maria replied I sure do, come on Mr. Russ, set down here and I'll fix you a plate, when he finished he was full as a tick.

Wade and Lola came in and set down beside him, Russ congratulated them told the they make a perfect couple, Wade asked "him a favor, he wanted to take Lola to the island, for a brief honeymoon."

Wade smiled "that's where she want's to go," Russ smiled, and said "that would be a perfect place."

Russ asked if he had talked to Gary about using the door? Wade said "I did and he said it was fine with him," Russ told "him not to take a location device with him," not until I get it on paper that the island is in our name, then he said "I'm sorry that island belong's to Lola as much as it does to the rest of us, but I do want to keep it in the family."

Wade smiled and said "Russ you can trust me, Russ replied I know that Wade, when are you going? Right now, Gary said to come on up when were ready.

Betsy asked Lola if the "girl's knew you were going to the island?" she smiled and said "it might be a good idea if they didn't know, because I'm sure they would want to go with you, Lola smiled and said "this one I'm not shearing."

Wade smiled, and said "just the two of us alone on a deserted island, that's every man's dream."

I didn't tell the Director, I was getting married, so he might come looking for me about the CIA business, so suger foot we had better get cracking Lola kissed him and said "let's go lover boy."

So Lola and Wade, Russ and Betsy headed for the compound, Gary Sr. was on duty to day, he smiled and said "here come's the bride and the heck with groom," just kidding Wade! Russ asked Wade to get some sample's of the oil on the island, the oil after refining was going to be run the generator's for the electrical system for the home, we planed to build.

Gary walked over to the door, and said "ok Russ take us to paradise, Russ put his hand Gary's and he opened the door, and they all stepped out on the Island, Wade said "you guy's weren't supposed to come, Russ said once you've been here to this magical place."

Gary smiled and said "Wade were just pulling your leg," Gary, Russ and Betsy turned, went back into the compound.

Russ, asked Gary "if he thought, getting the two CIA op's would change our status, about having to stay here, with you, it's not that staying here is so bad, it's that I had plain's for starting construction on our place in paradise."

Gary smiled then said "Russ I have no idea, what they have in mind for you and the island, but my experience with the FED'S is that if they get hold of you, there's no way out, I don't mean that in a harmful way, it's just when thay found out about our door, and what it did, every agency in the Government is using it, I'm not complaining of coarse, the door only works if Janice and I and our two children, operate it. and if what you've found on that island, does what I think it does, make's people younger, I'm already hooked on the water, I'm having the best sex I've ever had, and if the public every found out that it existed, who knows just how far they would go to have it."

Do you understand "what I'm saying," Russ said "yes, but if no body else knows where it at," Gary "that why you are here now, some one think's you know the location of the of the fountain of youth, that's why those two guy's from the CIA, came looking for you," Gary said "it really depends on how deeply that information, got into the system of the CIA.

And if Sandy can get to the bottom of this mess soon enough, that's how quickly you get away for here."

Russ asked "who is Sandy?" he's the director of the FBI, Gary said "I think Andrew will come to inquire, about the fountain of youth, Russ looked at him inquiringly," Gary said "what, oh Andrew, he's the President of the United States, he's the one who can get what you want, to own the island,"

Russ smiled and said "I think I had already figured that out, with you calling him the chief."

CHAPTER 20

Lola and Wade on the island by them self's, Lola asked what he wanted to do he smiled at her, what do you think, were on our honeymoon. there first day, was indeed a honeymoon, they stayed in the cave all day doing what come's naturally.

On second day, Lola took Wade all over the island, Wade gathered the oil samples, as they gathered their food.

Wade started looking for a place, Russ could build his home, Lola told him she thought, Russ wanted their home on top, of the waterfall, he asked if Russ could afford to build something like that, here, she told him about Russ selling his business, that she didn't know how much, he got out of it but Betsy had told her, he was a rich man! So between sessions with his beautiful wife.

He started planing what he would do, if he could build a home here, and he tried to see how every conceivable structure would look like. what he came up with was a clear acrylic dome over a flat structure, with sliding patricians for room's in side of it, standing on stilt's of steel or aluminum with stairs coming down from both side's of the waterfall. he finally told Lola, what he had been thinking, and she loved what he was seening.

So he drew what he saw, in his mind's eye, showed it to Lola, she was so pleased, she told him, she was going to show it to Russ.

That for this place it would be perfect, if wind's or foul weather came, it would slide right over it.

On their third day, they got a surprise, while doing it in the sand on the side of the lake.

Sandy and Andrew, Gary and Russ with Betsy and Janice came through the door, and it just so happened, it was the finishing up part, Wade saw them but he didn't stop. he and Lola were giggling like children, he picked her up and jumped into the lake, Sandy and the President were a little embarrassed at catching there ace agent in the throws, of passion, Gary and Janice, looked the same, when Russ and Betsy, saw that there guest, were a little red in the face, Russ started laughing, then he said "that's what mother nature intended for us to be doing in a paradise, like this," he and Betsy walked over to where Wade and Lola were in the water, shook out the towels they were laying on and helped them get out of the water with dignity."

When Wade and Lola were out of the water, and covered, they both hugged them, Russ whispered to "Wade way to go, I see you've been having fun!"

Wade replied "you've got that right, friend." they walked over to where Sandy, Andrew, Gary and Janice were still standing looking embarrassed, then Wade shook hand's with Andrew, Sandy, Gary and Janice, then introduced his wife to Andrew and Sandy, and they were very polite to her, she hugged them both and said any "friend's of my husband are friend's of mine."

Wade said "honey do you know who you just hugged?" no! Well Andrew is the Presedent of the United State's, Lola smiled and said "well I won't hold that against him" Wade honey, you must remember we were here for two year's, and we've only been back for, she looked at Betsy, what for four or five week's, Betsy smiled and said "five week's," Andrew smiled "I prefer what, she said first, that she wouldn't hold that aginst me!"

Wade said "I thought you guy's would becoming, but you surprised us let me and my lady go find our cloth's, and they scooted up to the cave."

Gary ask "Andrew if he had tried the water from the Island?" He said "no he hadn't," Russ got him a cup full from the water fall, he also got a cup full for Sandy, they each down the cup, and handed it back for more, they both, said "that's the best tasting water they've ever tasted." when they drank their third cup, Russ told them that the water was an aphrodisiacs that when they get back home, their wife's would notice a surge of sexual energy.

That they should take a gallon of it to give to their wife's, Sandy said "your just pulling our leg's, right?"

Wade and Lola were back with cloth's on, if you don't believe me ask Gary and Janice, or Wade and Lola, then Russ asked "Wade if he had some of the purple fruit, here?" he walked over to the edge of the lake, and pulled out a net bag, and with drew two of them, and handed them to Russ, he asked if they were hungry, Sandy said I could eat something, then he looked at the

President, what about you sir? he smiled and said "it's been a while sence I had breakfast! so sure I could eat," Russ took out his pocket knife and cut them a two inch slice, and handed it to them, Gary and Janice both said "they wanted some to," Wade and Lola had some.

But most of all, they were interested, in watching Andrew and Sandy they both had the strangest face, as they were eating, then they both started smiling and looking at each other, then Sandy said "that's my Mother's fried stake with mash potatoes, green bean's, and apple pie, then he said wow I've wanted that for so long, then a tear came to his eye, she's been dead for ten year's now," he sat down in the sand, Janice and Betsy sat down with him thinking he was going to cry, Sandy saw what they were doing, and said "no no I'm fine it's just that it bring such fond memories."

Andrew, the true politician, was munching away, they were expecting him to tell them what he was eating, he saw the look in their face's, then he said "you know those little fried chicken wing's, my wife give's me a fit every time I eat some, they give me such indigestion, but god are they good!"

Now he said "who's going to tell me, what I just had?" they all started laughting, Russ said "I Guess I should be the one, because the girl's and I lived on them for two year's, what we think is what ever you mind want's it tells you, your eating it, the taste the smells the goodness of what you want, in every aspect, but as you see it look's like a plain ordinary eggplant, I once thought we were in the gardan of eden, because, every thing we needed was provided for us, we had food, we found oil, that provided us with light at night, and eventually, we processed it into fuel for my plane, which got us back home."

Wade handed Russ his note book, showing a scale drawing of a dome home on top of the volcano looking structure, Russ said "that's would be perfect," then he asked were did you learn to how to do this, Wade replied when I was in school I first thought, I wanted to be an architect, but the FBI soon changed my mind."

Russ said "I think we could use this, have it prefabricated and bring it to the island and assemble it." he showed it to Betsy, she thought it was perfect and you could always's see out side.

Gary told "Russ he had a two hundred gallion tank, lined with porcelain to keep from contaminating the water to keep it pure, while you are showing Andrew and Sandy the island, can I fill it up, if that's alright with you.

Russ, sure, I've already told Sandy and the President, that they should take a gallion home with them because they will be horney dud's, to give to their wife's so they can match their libido's with their's, Gary said "you told them that," Russ laughed, and said "it worked for you didn't it," Gary smiled and said "it did indeed."

Gary went threw the door, and in a little while was back with a two inch hose and put it into the lake, Russ walked back over to where the President Wade, Sandy and Janice, Lola and Betsy were talking, the President asked what's "Gary doing, Russ told him, he was filling a tank at the compound with water from the lake," and that "I was to show you around the island, so where do you want to start," Andrew said "I'd like to see where the fruit is growing, then he asked Russ if he could get a cutting to see if he could get to grow in Virginia I have a hot house there, I would think that maybe the condition's would be the same, my wife grow's orchid's and it has to be moist for them to grow!"

Russ, thought about it for a minute, "well sir I don't mind you getting a cutting as long as it doesn't kill the tree."

Wade smiled and said "we brought some zip lock bag's and some paper towel's and as long as you can keep it moist, it might work."

Then Russ said "if you will follow me, and Betsy honey if you would bring up the rear, I'll put Lola and Wade in the middle, who by the way have been here three day, and of coarse Lola was here with us for two year's, when they got to where the hole was into the cave, he got on his knee's and went in and told Andrew to follow him in, when they were all in, it was a little dark Wade told them he had refurbished the torche's just today and ignited four of them, and the glow Russ had remembered came to life, he said honey do you remember, Betsy and Lola both said they did, and Lola put her hand over her mouth, Wade hugged her, that's ok love." the President said "how green this is, it look's like carpet, the whole place look's like it's covered with carpet," he and Sandy sat down on the raised portion then laid down on it, Betsy said "that's where we all slept, and it was quiet comfortable for us.

Sandy said "why would you build, this is prefect, the way it is," Russ smiled then said "it is that, but I can afford to build something much better, and with oil, we could process it into fuel for generator's for electricity," he ask Sandy if he had looked at the drawing that Wade did, they would be perfect for what I want?

He replied no, but I'm not sure I like Wade, being an architect, he's the best FBI agent we have, we've never given him a case, that he couldn't solve

Russ looked at him and said "I'm sure he is, but he's married now, and he might like to slow down, a little, I know that if he's willing I'm going to get him to help me, with what he's dreamed up for us to built, he and his wife will own part of it.

Sandy looked at him, then called Wade over, Russ is telling me that you might want to quit the FBI, Russ said "I didn't say that," I only said "I wanted him to help me with building our dream home here, sence it will be his to."

Wade looked at Russ, said "really," Russ said "sure Lola was with us on the plane when we accidentally found this island." but I want the island to be called Willow island, Wade smiled and said "I have no problem with that, then he looked at Sandy, I'm not quiting the agency but if Russ will let me, I'm building what I envisioned, should be here, do you have a problem with that."

Sandy said "we should talk about it later," Andrew joined in and said "let him build his dream, he is staying with the Pepper's anyway, he can come and go easily through the door."

Wade said "thanks Mr. President, you will always's be able to come and go also, right Russ? he replied sure!

Betsy said "we had better get moving, we've been here for at least thirty minutes, we should get on with the tour, so they all left the cave, and headed down the other side of the mountain, and in a short while, they were all at the orchard, Wade had brought a net bag to pick a few for them to take home

Andrew, started looking for a place on the tree's he could cut, for his planting that wouldn't harm the tree's."

Russ lead them, from there on down to the beach, when they got there he explained that the island was round, and the beach was perfect for walking or running for the exercise.

Andrew said "he thought it would be perfect for that, boy would I like this just for the privacy," Janice we "need this along with, Stony Knob,"

Janice laughed and said "Andrew you should have seen me the last time we were here, we had a ball in the lake." they walked around until they came to the small river coming from the lake and followed it back up to the lake.

Gary was swimming in the lake in the nude, he was surprised, when he saw them coming, hurred out of the water, they saw him naked, they whisled at him, as he was hurring into his pant's he mooned them, and that cracked them all up. when they all had there fun, Andrew said "we need to leave, or at least I do the boy's will be wondering where I am, but you guy's can stay as long as you can, but I would like to set down with you Russ,

Gary and Wade, to see what kind of deal we can work out, about the Island.

So if you guy's go with me, back to Gary's place, we will have time to do it this afternoon, he looked at Russ, Gary and Wade, you think we could do that, they all agreed."

Gary had his tank full of water from the lake, and he had filled two gallon's each for Sandy and Andrew, when they were all back in the compound, Gary asked Andrew where should we talk, he said let's go to my qrarters, there will be less ear's to hear. when they all got settled into the President's den, Russ was marveling at how comfortable, the room was, he had conceived it to be a little more ornate than it was, it was a man's room, leather furniture.

As he was setting down on one of the couches, he told the President, he really liked his pad.

Gary, Wade, Russ and Andrew, then he told Wade," he had sent Sandy back to Washington, that he didn't need to set in on out discussion."

Then he turned to Russ, and said "I don't blame you for not telling anyone where that paradise is, and I think you should keep it that way, because who knows just how the world would react to the fountain of youth, so you should keep that location a secret, what I would like, if Gary agrees of coarse, is that you and he and Wade work through the door, to achieve what you want, for a home there."

CHAPTER 21

Russ smiled at Wade, I think he just gave us the go-a-head to getting started.

Wade said "I think we should get a Japanese construction company, they make some strong acrylic's, we'll need that for the dome." we'll need some equipment for processing the oil into fuel, for the generators and I think we'll need at least three, very strong one's at that."

Gary spoke up and said "I can see that you guy's are ready to get started."

Andrew said "I can talk to Norosokie, he can give us some good company's to do the job."

Russ said "I'll have to give up the location, what about that?" Wade said "if we can get what I'm thinking about, build it there, take it apart, bring it to the island and reassemble, it shouldn't take long, to put it back together and if Andrew would let us have the core of engineer's, to assemble it, at a price of coarse, we get it delivered by the company who's building it, to bring it to the island, off load it, and leave, we could send the engineer's, through through the door, to assemble, of coarse we'll need cranes, we may even have to build road to get to the site."

Russ made a face, "I don't want to change the island that much, maybe we could design a new kind of crane, Gary said "let me and my son's tackle that one, we have come up with some really good idea's in the past, give me the general idea of what you need."

Russ drew what he was thinking of, showed it to Gary, he said "that sound's like it would work, I think if we can do this we may have a new design for a crane."

Andrew chuckled and said "you guy's are smart," Russ smiled and said "I know a guy, that might just want to invest, in a company like that, Mr. President you might know him, I think he's one of you bigest financial campaign supporter's, do you know Jeff Hobart, he thought for a moment then said "yes, and I think he's one of he richest men in this country, if not the world."

Andrew smiled and said "and you know him? Russ said I sure do, he is one of the nicest people, you ever want to know!"

Andrew scratched his head, "can you call him now?" Russ smiled said "I sure can, right now, Wade handed him a phone form an end table, he punched in the numbers, when someone answered the phone, and said this is the Hobart resident, Russ asked if this was Larry, yes sir it is, Russ told him who he was, and asked if his dad was there? No sir he's at the cottage with Mom, could you transfer down there? Yes sir, hang on just a moment, when someone answered the phone in the cottage, it sounded like Mary, Russ told her who he was, she said "hi Russ we've been trying to get hold of you for several day's, to invite you and Betsy over for that swim, Jeff and I both in joyed your company," well Mary we are in the mountains, with some old friend's.

Is Jeff there, yes he is, would you let me talk to him please, she said "Just a moment Russ!" Jeff picked up the phone and said "hi Russ, where are you? I've talk to Bobby and Bo, they told me that the FBI had you hidden somewhere, all they could say, was something about the fountain of youth it all sounded so weird, but I was getting concerned, about you," Russ said "well Jeff I think we're ok, but what I called you about was I'm setting with someone you might know, Russ looked at the President and asked if he wanted to talk? He indicated that he did, Jeff let me introduce you to and old friend's of ours."

Andrew "hi Jeff how are you," Jeff said "Andrew Mellon, how are you?"

Andrew just fine!" Jeff said "let me tell you what my son told me this morning at breakfast, he told me that I would be talking to the President of the United State's at six o'clock this after noon."

Andrew said "well my watch say's six on the dot," Jeff told him about his son's ability to see the future, that it was a gift from his Grandfather Adam's

Andrew said "Russ knows where you live, yes he dose, and were just seting on the porch at the cottage eating some of Lucille's finest ice cream,"

Andrew said "my favorite ice cream," Jeff said "well sir we've got plenty if you were here you could have some.

Andrew said "hold to that thought, were close!" hung up the phone, OK guy's were going to have ice cream.

Russ said "what about the girl's," Andrew replied "I don't think we should over whelm the Hobart's on our first visit," Russ said "sir but if my wife find's out that I've had ice cream at the Hobart's, I'm a dead man."

Andrew chuckled, and said "well we can't have that, so I suspect we better get the ladies," Gary called the house, and told Janice, Betsy and Lola to come up to the compound, were going to get some ice cream!" they were there in a few minute's, Sabrina and Brent were maning the the door.

Brent told them "there were two more arrivals expected in at seven thirty."

Sabrina said "Pop after that you got it, because I'll be gone," Gary said "I can handle it babe," Gary put his hand on the door and told "Russ to put his hand on his, you know where we're going."

And Gary opened the door and they all stepped out on the pattio of the Hobart's, Jeff jumped up at first, then laughed and said "you scared the bejesus out of me."

Russ laughed, and said "I could only think of the deck as a point of entry." then said "I'll let Gary explain, how we did this, it's beyond my understanding." he turned to Gary, this is "Jeffery Hobart and his lovely wife Mary," "they already know Betsy, this is the President of the united States, I think you already know him, and this is Janice Gary's lovely wife and this is Wade Hound, and his lovely wife Lola." they all shook hand's, and Mary got them all a place to set, then the ladie's all went into the cottage to get some more ice cream.

Jeff said "Andrew do you mind if I call my family down to introduce you to them, I know it would be a thrill for them."

Andrew said "I would really like to me you son, what you told me about his ability to see the future, intrigued me, because Gary has a door, that will take you any where you want to go, and Russ has the fountain of youth, and you have a son able to see the future, that's is a triple bit of good luck for a President."

Jeff looked at him, and said "Gary Pepper has a door that will take you anywhere you wish to go, and Russ has found the fountain of youth, and this is all true," Andrew smiled then said "it all sound's crazy I know, but it's all true." when Russ called you we were all in the mountain's just out side of Ashville in a place called Stoney Knob, and we just walked from there to your deck, ask Gary, Gary smiled and said "I know how you feel, I inherited it from an Uncle I never knew, with a right tidy some of money, he and my aunt found it in England, and had it for about a year and half, before they knew what they really had, my aunt bought it for the beautiful carving it had on it, she was a world class cardiologist, and my uncle was a lawyer who owned his own law firm in Ashville, and they both could read Latin, and as I gather they figured out what was written on the door that Merlin the Magican had created it in the later part of King Arther rein, right after the fall of Camelot and I know you think, that sound's crazy, but the entire federal government use's it all the time, for stealth purpose's," Gary looked at Andrew, "tell him Andrew, he smiled and said "the best way for me to travel," Jeff smiled at Russ, is this all true? Russ smiled back at him and said "if I lieing I'm dieing."

Just then, the ladies came out passing around the ice cream, Mary told the "President that this is some of Lucille's best, as a surprise you will meet the lady who make's this delicious, ice cream," just as she said that, two J—deer cart's pulled to the side of the cottage, and in a few second's John Lucille, Bob and June with Larry came up the step's.

Jeff stood and "introduced them to the President, the rest of them," the President, said "this is the fine lady who make's this ice cream possible for the World to enjoy," Lucille thanked him, said "I don't personally make it anymore, but I make sure that our company make's it like I did."

He smiled and said "just as long as you keep on making it," he turned and said "right" Gary replied "your are right about that," and they all set around enjoying the ice cream. until they couldn't eat anymore, Andrew asked Larry if he and his dad could go into the cottage, and talk for a few minutes.

Larry smiled and said "dad do we do this," Jeff smiled, said "son I could listen to what he has to say" but I don't think he understand's that you already know what he's going to say, Andrew smiled and said "well son what's your answer," Larry said well sir let me talk to the family and see what they think about what you purpose."

Andrew smiled then said "I couldn't ask for anymore, and shook Larry and Jeff's hand." all the ladies, were in the cottage, cleaning, the ice cream bowl's, Jeff started to tell John and Bob, about what Russ and Gary, then the President said

Jeff that's privileged information, and not to be discussed, he looked at Larry "do you understand? Yes sir I do!"

Wade said "Andrew I think we should go, we wouldn't want to ware out our welcome."

Jeff replied "you couldn't do that, your welcome here any time you have the time to come, he turned to Russ, and you young man, we have a swimming date," Mary's asked me "if you and Betsy were coming?"

Russ said "I would like that, and if I can get our friend Gary to assist in that Endeavour,"

Wade pulled Jeff aside and asked "if he could get his family in side so we could leave quietly?"

Jeff looked at Larry and said "can you handle it, "yes sir," in few minutes he had his grandparent's headed up the hill, Wade smiled and said "that young man is sharp as a tack," Jeff said "that young man has two PHD's one from Harvard the other from MIT."

"So you can say, he is sharp as a tack, "wow, he is indeed a brilliant, young man!" When Andrew, saw the grandparent's leave, he told "Wade we should leave."

Gary ask "let me take Jeff and Mary, back to our place, just for a little bit of coarse, if they would like to go, Jeff looked at

Mary, she smiled and said "Jeffery, I want to see there place," Jeff "what the boss want's, she gets."

Gary said "is every one ready to go, and he opened the door, the President went in first, and he told Jeff and Mary to go next, they seemed hesitant at first until Betsy took Mary's hand and lead her into the compound, Jeff was holding her other hand and in with her, Russ, Wade, Lola and Gary next"

Jeff and Mary were looking around rather amazed, at seeing where they were, Jeff said "where are we?" Gary said "you are in the Presidental compuund at Stony Knob, N. C., Andrew built it when he found out what the door can do."

Andrew said "Gary I need to get back to Washington to night I need to see my wife, Gary ask if "Russ, Betsy, Jeff and Mary could peak into the Oval Office Andrew smiled and said "I don't see why not," Gary opened the door they all walked into the Oval office, Russ, Betsy, Jeff and Mary, were in aw of what they were seening, Jeff said "you know I have one of the best charter service's in the State's and in the World for that matter. and we just walked threw a door, in Adamsville to Stony Knob N. C. from there to the White House, in DC. with none other than the President of the United State's, this is surely a magical day," Gary smiled and said "that's it Magic." the President, walked around his desk, opened a bottom draw. pulled out two photographs, signed them and said "remember me in the next election and smiled," then said "just kidding, it's just a memento of your visit to the White House, then he picked up the phone, punched in a number, "hi honey see you in ten minutes top's" hung up phone, and said "next time we do this you have to come for dinner, with me and my wife."

Gary said "thanks Andrew, it's alway's a pleasure to be with you, Andrew smiled and said "Gary your faimly, and I hope Jeff and Mary and Russ, and Betsy, will become family to.

CHAPTER 22

Andrew shook all their hand's, and told "Jeff, to let him know if Larry will help me take care of some problem's, in two branches of the government, and if he is willing to help me, I wouldn't take up to much of his time, of coarse with both of your approval. he looked a Mary then at Jeff and said "thanks for listening to me." they all went back to Stony Knob, Gary said "let me take you down to the house, I know you have the best ice cream, but I know where the best

French apple pie is made," he lead them out of the compound, to the golf cart's and down to the house, Jeff and Mary were very inpressed with Gary's home, he lead them into the kitchen, Janice and Maria had warm

French apple pie, waiting for them, with a scoop of Lucille best ice cream, they all sat down, Mary said "Jeff if we could steal Maria form the Peppers, we could corner the market on this pie," then she looked a Janice and said "I'm just kidding, but I think you could market this real well.

I help Lucille in her business, and they truly have made a fortune, with the ice cream."

Janice said "it's something to think about, but we've got a lot going on around here, with Gary and the boy's in the munition industry. and Merlin door, Gary and I, Sabrina our daughter, and son Gary Jr. are the only one's that can get the door, to work, and sometimes it work's us to much, at first the whole federal government, was shuttling through to place's all over the world. until Gary had a talk with Andrew, about it, and he is now only scheduling high priority thing's, through it."

So we can use it for ourself's, like in the beginning, it belong's to us, we inherited from Gary's uncle." then she looked at Wade, "until this dude showup with his FBI badge caused all kind's of problem's, but now he's a loved member of our family.

Now that he's married Lola I think I see a sparkle in his eye's or is it the water from Willow island, and before you leave take some with you and test it out and see what you think about it."

Jeff asked, "is that the water from the fountain of youth, that Russ discovered?"

Russ smiled and said "test it out, and tell me what you think, when we were stranded on the island, we were all in our late fifty's, how old do you think I am, now? Mary said "I thought you were in your thirty's, Betsy look's like a teenager to me.

Betsy said "thank you Mary, that's quite a complement for a sixty one year old women."

Russ said "she is like a teenager in bed, Betsy slapped him on his arm, Russ you staying with the Pepper's, be nice!"

All at the table chuckled at that, Jeff smiled and said, "give us at least four gallon of that stuff," Mary said "Jeffery Hobart your going to get a knot on your head, Buster!"

Wade said "he's right about what he telling you, then he asked Janice if she had any of the purple fruit still in the house, she thought, I think there is let me give them a taste, and see what they think!"

She got a plate from the refrigerator, took off the plastic wrap, there were four slices, she cut one of them in half, put them on a napkin for each of them.

Jeff said "what am I supposed to do with this, it looks like an uncooked eggplant, all at the table were looking at them, "what!" Jeff said, Mary said "they want your reaction of what it taste like," they both took a bite

Mary looked at Jeff, and he at her, she smiled, "you remember the trip around the world, with Mom and Dad, Lucille and John the beef Wellington on the ship when I was carring Larry around in my tummy," Jeff smiled, you ate it like you were starving, honey, "well that is what I'm tasting, right now

Jeff said "I'm tasting something Martha used to feed me, when I was a child and holy cow I haven't tasted it, for such a long time, do you remember those oval Johnny cake, she would put peanut butter, slice bananas sprinkle sugar on them, and at that time in my life they were the best the very best."

Then they stoped and looked at the rest of them looking at them, Mary smiled and said "what in the world is this stuff, I know it's not beef Wellington, but why is it tasting like it?"

Jeff smiled and said "I know what you mean honey!"

Jeff said "OK who's going to tell me what we just had," Russ smiled and said, "that's what we ate on the island, and what ever we wanted mentally that's what we ate."

"All I can tell you is that it give's, you what you want to eat! how I don't know! But I know where they grow.

Along with water that make you young, it on an uncharted, Island, and I know where its at, it's hard to belive I know, but it all true."

Jeff said "honey I think it's time we left," Russ let's sat down and talk about this island."

Gary and Janice you have a beautiful home, and a fantastic way to travel and I want some of that water to take home."

Gary, Russ and Betsy took them back up to the compound, Gary gave them four gallon's of Island water, and asked them to "let us know, what you think of it."

Mary said "we have some old folk's at home who could benefit, drinking it," Jeff said "we'll try it on Martha, first, if she perks up, we'll try on the out law's, sorry honey, the in law's," Mary whacked him.

Gary told Jeff "to put his hand on his arm and think were he want's to go," and he opened the door into the cottage, Russ helped them get the water through the door, and they said "goodnight."

Gary told "Russ and Betsy goodnight, left the compound, Russ and Betsy went to their quarter's found the girl playing card's, and joined them, it wasn't long before they were playing strip poker, Russ figured the ladies were all a little frisky, and he didn't get to sleep until three in the morning with a smile on his face. when Jeff and Mary finally road up to the house, with the water, and into the basement, and up the stair's, Jeff saw Martha puttering around in the kitchen he got a glass, and filled it with water for one of the jug's, and told her to "drink it," she "I don't need any water," Jeff said "you drink it now, before I put you across my knee," she smiled and said "you and what army is going put me across you knee's," Jeff said "listen to me, this has some minerals in it that's suppose to make you feel better, and I want you to drink it for me Mom," she hugged him and said "anything for my baby."

She down the glass, "wow that's good water, then asked "for more," that time she said, "my toe's to the top of my head are tingling."

Jeff smiled I told you it would make you feel better, she hugged him picking him up off the floor, she smiled and said "I haven't been able to do that in a few year's."

Jeff said "I'm putting the rest of this gallon, in the fridge, and you drink it or answer to me." she smiled, "I will son," he and Mary left the kitchen, and went into the den where Bob, June, John and Lueille reading, Mary had gotton four plastic cup's Jeff had a gallon of water, poured a cup full and handed one to John and one to each of them.

June asked "what's this," Jeff said "it's a new meneral water I've found, I want you to try it, and tell me what you think?" when they drank it, they looked at each other and Lucille asked "did it make you tingle." they all smiled and said "it did indeed" and held there cup's up for more, Jeff refilled all four cup's

Larry walked into the room, when he saw the gallon jug in his father's hand he said "Dad you got some of the water, didn't you?"

Jeff smiled and said "you know don't you son!" Yes dad I do, and I think these old fogies are perfect subject's."

"Dad I need to talk to you and mom, about what the President want's me to do for him, can we go into the library, and talk," Jeff said "sure son, your Mom and I want to help you any way we can, I've allway's worried that you have to much on your mind," Larry smiled and said "dad Grandpaw tought me how to handle what goes throuth my brain, how to compartmentalize my thought's and how to throw out the garbage."

So the gift "I have is truly a gift, so don't worry for me, Grandpaw worries more about you than he dose about me. he still want's me to help you, he love's you, and belive it or not he has loved you from day one, when he first saw your tiny face, and knew you were like him, when you were young he thought he was molding you for the future."

Larry reached across the table, and patted his father hand, then said "I think he did a fine job, Dad!" when Mary saw the tear's in Jeff's eye's, she took both their hand's and said "I love my boy's," now let's get down to business, she asked what have you decide about the Presidend request, Larry said "well Mom he want's me to tell him who's leaking information, from the FBI, to the CIA, that's why Mr. Willow is staying at Stony Knob, it's a fortress, because of the door, and what Russ has discovered on his island."

"He want's me to work with Wade Hound, one of the best agent's the FBI has, I think I would like to do it, now what are your thought's."

Jeff looked at Mary, she said "no way young man, unless they can assure me you will be completely safe!"

Larry said "Mom I know I will be safe, somebody in the FBI is leaking information to the CIA, I think I can tell who or what is doing it, as soon as I get there, dad do you have Wade's number at the Pepper's, let me talk to him and get a feeling from him, what he think's."

I have decided I would like to look into the problem, and correct it for the President."

He looked at his Mother, smiled and said, "George want's me to find somebody for him, there is nothing for us, in this area."

She looked at Jeff, wondering if he remembered, who George was, he didn't act like he did, she punched him, did you hear what he said? "yes love!"

What are you saying son, Larry looked at him, and said "ask Mom, Dad she can enlighten you," on what I'm saying, Mary said "Jeffery Martin Hobart think about who George is, a surprised look came to his face, "oh, sorry son your mother introduced me to him, when you were little, you and I were having so much fun jumping off he big rock, before the cottage was built. then he looked at Larry, I thought you were sexually active, looking for the right one, you know your mother and I will except who ever you choose to spend the rest of you life with."

Mary said "he's what! young man," I thought you were just dating, all those cute girl's, Larry said "Mom you remember when you were young, and you and Dad first met, and how it was between you two."

Love between two people, (to love and be loved, is the greatest gift on earth).

I don't think you could, dispute that, Mary smiled and said "no son I couldn't, you know we want every thing for you in this life. Jeff smiled and said "is grandpaw bugging you about filling up this old house, Larry chuckled, you know about that?"

Jeff smiled and said "at first that was my job!" did I not ever show you the letter he left me, he had written it before he died, telling me that he wanted me to fill this old house with children, just watching Me and Larry growing up brought love and life back to this old place, and that it was my duty to fill this old house, with children."

Larry said "Dad I want to see it sometime," now, I still want to help Wade with our quest, I think I know already, what's happing at the FBI office's in D.C. and Grandpaw told me that I would find my Gracie, in that endevor.

Mary smiled and said "son I think you should go," She giggled and said "now that would be a fine pair George and Gracie Hobart, Jeff chuckled, our son rattling all over this house.

Larry said "you guy's stop it, and you better not tell my Grandpaw's and Grandmaw's, Grandpaw John would rag me to death, so please don't tell them, please!"

Mary and Jeff both just cackled, and finally Mary said "son we wouldn't put you in that place."

Larry looked at his watch and said "I don't think I should call tonight, so I will call tomorrow."

Mary and Jeff went to bed, Larry right behing them, and when thing's got quiet, they didn't stay quiet for long, such moaning and groaning, coming from Bob and June bedroom, John and Lucille was just as bad!

Larry bedroom was just across from Bob and June room, he knocked on his Mom and Dad's bedroom then opened it, his Mother was getting out of bed he told "her she should check the old folk's, it sound's like there sick," Jeff found his rob and put it on, Jake was partially aroused, so Jeff attempted to cover him up, and they were in the hall way and Mary started to open her Mother's door, Jeff stopped her, honey, "that's not moaning, he pulled Larry & her close to the door, and said "listen, those old folk's are having a very good time, Larry snickered, his Mother put her hand over his mouth, and said "hush."

She opened his door, and said "go to sleep your day will come," he replied yes Mother, "Dad's rob's is pointing north, you better go take care of it,"

"son I was in the process of doing just that, when you knocked on our door "sorry Mom, I knew what was going on, I think the water you and Dad gave them turned them on, and I just wanted you to hear what I was hearing.

"Sorry again," he kissed her on her cheek, and said "good night Mom! the next morning, Bob, June, Lucille and John were all smile's at the breakfast table, Martha seemed to be happy to, as they were eating old Dr. Wilcox came into the room with his rob and slipper's on, when Martha saw him come into the room, she shuffled him a place at the table, and all eye's were on them, when she saw them looking, listen you people, I asked him to move in with me last night, and that sweet man, did."

She looked at Jeff, then said "don't say a word, young man, I can still turn you over my knees."

Jeff busted out laughting, and said "no mom, I know my place around here," and to see my momma happy, with someone as special as that old saw bone's!

All I can say is love is in the air, and isn't it delicious," Larry said "Dad I think you should buy the well, that water is coming from." then he looked at all his grandparent's, "you guy's, grunting, moaning, like teenager's just how was I suppose to sleep, oh yes when I heard Grandpa John whaling like a banshee, I finally had to put a pillow over my head to get to sleep." all four of them started laughing, Bob said "Jeffery if you can buy that well, please do so, right away!"

Jeff smiled and said "I can't buy it dad, but I'll try to get you a visit to where the water came from, I think it's somewhere in the Pacific ocean.

John said "there's no more," Jeff said "dad, there's more, I'll just have to get it from a friend of mine!"

At ten-fourty Larry called Gary Pepper house, and asked "to speak to Wade Hound," and after a couple of transfer's, Wade finally answered the Phone

Larry told him who he was, and that the President wanted you and I to work on a problem, he has!

Wade said "he told me about talking to you, are we ready to start! Yes sir,

"where are you going to pick me up at here or at the cottage, Wade said "I'll have to get Russ, you met him at the cottage, he know's where you live be at the cottage, pack a few thing's, that will make you comfortable sence I don't know how long you will be here."

"Let your Mom and Dad know you coming with us ok! "Yes sir!"

"what time do you want me to be at the cottage?" Larry let's say one oclock

I'll have to get Russ, to help Gary get to where you are, Larry said "I'll see you at one," and flip his cell phone closed.

CHAPTER 23

Larry went to tell his Mom and Dad, that he would be leaving at one o'clock his Mother was standing close, dreading to hear that her son would be gone for a while, Jeff walked up behind her, what are you doing honey, she hugged him, "you know how Mother's are, they never want to let go of their baby's."

I know love, "but he's no longer a child, the smartest young man I know!

And I don't think Grandpaw, would let him get into any kind of danger, I know I checked up on Mr. Hound and he is the best they've got at the FBI so I know he'll be alright, we can't let the old folk's know, that he will be gone for a few day's.

Larry walked up to them and said "ok what are we discussing, you son"

"Dad."

"I know son, you Mother, if she knew the first time we jumped off our rock, it never would have happened, so sometime's we shouldn't tell her what going on, right son," "yes

Dad, but that's the nature of being a Mom and I'm glad she is mine!"

Wade told "me to be at the cottage at one o'clock, he told me to pack comfortably and if I need anything else I'm sure I could get it in Washington."

"Just let me go to the cottage alone!" "I would son but the old folk's drank all the water, and I would like to refill them again, is that ok with you."

"Sure Dad, but Mom doesn't need to come?" "Right son."

Jeff and Larry were setting with their feet dangling off the big rock when Wade, Russ and Gary came through the door, Gary noticed the empty water bottles thought about filling them, then he saw Larry and Jeff setting on the big rock and they all walked down to where they were setting, Jeff told them to have a seat, Russ said "that sound's like a winner to me," Wade and

Gary did the same, Jeff told them "to relax and enjoy the peacefulness of Adam's manor." they sat listening to the water running past as Jeff and his family had for many year's, Russ asked "who put the brass plaque, with Jeff, Mary, Larry's place on it."

Jeff said "Russ that not brass, that is one hundred percent Pure gold" Russ said "wow, I bet that cost you a pretty," Jeff said "do you think I can't afford a little gold."

Russ laughed and said "sorry Jeff I know you can afford any thing you want!" Jeff said "this place is something very special, to me, my wife and this young man, he ruffled Larry hair, Larry said Dad! That's why the cottage is here, when I was a young man, I loved this place, Mary love it to, Larry and I skinny dipped here, when he was in diaper's to me it's just the a perfect place to be, he look at Wade, you take good care of my son, do you understand, Wade said "yes sir, I do."

Larry got up, and said "Mr. Hound I think we should go, before my Dad make you sign an affidavit to that affect, Wade smiled, "son I think you are lucky to have a father that feel's that way." Russ said "Larry you should be thankful to have a father that love's you that much."

Larry said "I'm truly grateful, I have four grandparents, who are super, and Martha, that's a moma to me," Jeff said wait a minute "Martha is my Moma so she is you grandma."

Larry got up and started walking to the cottage, and they all followed him

Wade shook Jeff's hand, and said "he will be just fine, I'll see to it!"

Gary asked if he needed a few more jug's, Jeff said "I have six old people who had a ball last night, after drinking that water."

Gary smiled and said "it does have that effect on us old folk's."

When he opened the door, they all went into the compound, Gary filled the four gallons and gave him two more, and helped him set it on the deck, and, told him about getting himself a two hundred gallon tank, maybe you should do that to, we can get it out of the lake on Willow island.

Jeff hugged his son.

But Larry had spoted a girl talking to another woman at a desk, Wade noticed it and asked him if he wanted to be introduced, "to the pretty girl," Larry eye's lite up, "yes sir I do," Wade smiled well come on they walked over to where Sabrina and Erin was standing.

Wade said hi, "this is Dr. Larry Hobart, he wanted to meet your daughter he turned to Larry, this is Erin Messer, and her Mother Sabrina, she's Gary's daughter, Larry asked "if he could hugg her," Erin looked at him smiled and said "sure."

As he hugged her, he knew, this was his Gracie, George was excited but Larry wouldn't let him respond, that would come later, as they looked into each other's eye's they both knew, this was it.

He also hugged Sabrina, and told them how happy, he was to meet them,

Wade, saw the look's in their eye's. then he said "Doc, we need to get to the Hover building, are you ready," he smiled at them both and said "I'll see you guy's later."

Gary asked where to fella's, I thought the President.s office, Wade told him "we need to go to the Hover building first!"

Wade and Doc walked into the hallway just outside the director of the FBI's office, Wade told "the receptionist, that Sandy was expecting them," she picked up a phone, told him that "Wade was here," she said "you may go in"

Sandy was on the phone, talking to the President, he said "yes sir they are here, how do you want me to handle this, "ok yes sir."

CHAPTER 24

Sandy hung up his phone, "hi Wade this must be Larry Hobart," Wade said "this young man hold's two Doctorate's Degree's from two prestigious, school's," Oh Sandy said "I didn't know that, the President didn't tell me you were so well educated, he told me to give you all the support you needed for the task ahead."

Doc smiled and said "let's just say I know a lot of stuff, and I think I can solve your problem's."

If you will allow me to do so, Larry asked" how long ago did you check your office phone system, for bug's, Wade told me that he only report's to you and to the President. would you let me break down that phone, on your desk," Sandy smiled and said "I think that phone totally safe."

Larry smiled then said, "are you telling me I can't do it," Sandy looked at Wade for conformation on his decision, Wade said "sir I just heard you telling the President that you would give Doc your full support, and the first thing he ask for, your telling him no!"

Doc said "if you want let me look at it get one of your people, and let me watch him do it."

Sandy pondered what Doc was saying, Larry said "let me talk to the President, if he doesn't want my help, I can go back home," Wade said

"Sir I don't think you want to piss Andrew off, and what Doc want's is to look inside your phone.

So what damage could that do, Larry said "sir I have a PHD. from MIT, so if your worried I can't put it back together, call an expert, but for me it would be very simple.

I only thought that with so many new gadgets, being put on the market and black market, some of these thing's you wouldn't believe are so small and much more capable, but I guess your guy's would know, all about that, and probably developed most of them."

Doc said "if we could get another phone, so you still have the service,

Sandy, responded quickly, provideing Doc, with all he needed, he had the phone apart, he found what he was looking for, he showed it toWade, and then to Sandy, now you need to figure out how and who put this in your system and who is listening."

Wade told Sandy "we should put something fantastic out there, and see who take's the bate."

Doc, Wade followed the transmission, found a recording device on the first floor of the Hover building, in a bank of mail boxes, then found out, who had access to the box. they recorded that Wade had access to alien technology, the next day the mailman, who serviced that bank of mailbox's, took out a tape of the recording they had planted, the FBI pick him up, as soon as he put the tape into another box that he didn't service, the envelope was addressed to Langley Va. they questioned the mailman for hour's and finally concluded, he was only doing it for the extra money, he didn't know who paid him, but a seven hundred check came every month, and he had five kid's to feed and cloth so he didn't question, his benefactor, and was grateful to get the extra money. they couldn't find that he broke the law, he paid tax's on the money he received, Wade and Doc, told him that he wouldn't be getting the money for to much longer, and that if any one contacted him, he should let them know, they buged his cell and home phone to make sure, if anyone contacted him, they would know. they also bugged the envelope that the tape was in and they had an appointment with the Director of the CIA, Sandy asked the "President to make the appointment, and thought he mite be there also, Wade and Doc both had a device that would pick up the signal of the envelope, that had a radius three thousand yd's., something Doc had developed the short time he was in Washington, which dazzled every one at the FBI, they all wanted him to patent it, he asked "Wade if he wanted to do it, that he didn't need money.

Wade said "sure he would do it," Doc gave him all the specificataion's of his project.

As Wade and he were headed to Langley Virgina, they were to meet Sandy at the gate at the CIA Headquarter's, when they got there, they parked in a public parking area, close to the gate.

Sandy wasn't there yet, and Wade asked Doc if he would like to be an FBI agent, Doc chuckled, and said "Wade my faimly would kill me if I even thought about it, beside's, I work for my Dad, he has sport's team's and he's into computer's, and we still have a thriving Textile business, to handle it all! he even has his own personal bank!

So he's grooming me for the day, when I'll have to take over, and I have some pretty big shoe's to fill."

Just then Sandy's car pulled up behind them and he motioned for them get into his limo, when they were seated, they were quiet until they stopped at the entrance of the building.

Sandy went in first, with Wade and Larry just behind him, as soon as they were in the building, Larry and Wade sliped an earpiece into their right ear, that would let them hear the device, hanging on the loop of there of pant's. it wasn't long before they started hearing, a low resonance sound coming from somewhere close by, the further they walked down the hallway the louder the signal became.

Until they came to an open area, with six low cubical's in the middle, and six office's on each side, the cubical's were occupied, with four women and two men, Larry thought them to be personal assistants for the office personal, but the sound was coming from an older gentleman's section of the cubical.

Doc asked "Wade if he had picked up on where the signal was coming from, he replied not yet," Larry motioned to him to look at the mature gentleman in the cubical on the far side, when he zeroed in on him, he smiled and whispered "that's our man."

CHAPTER 25

Sandy had stopped and talking to someone, a little further down the hallway and when they got closer, it was the President Wade walked up and shook his hand, when Andrew saw Larry with him, he smiled and said "I've been hearing good thing about you young man," Larry smiled and said "I hope they've all been good sir," Andrew smiled and said "they've been very good

Sandy tells me you've invented and developed a new listening device. how's that working, Wade said "we've already found what we came for sir" would you like to see, sure Wade said "follow me, they walked back to the cubical's Wade lead them around to where the mature man was setting at his desk, Wade said "this is where the envelope with the tape," as he looked at the man name plate, John Wilson, he told him to stand up, he stood up looking puzzled, the President said "maybe we should get the Director of the CIA, Harry Ward out here."

When he showed up Andrew told him, that Wade had planted a bug in an envelope with tape from Sandy phone, "do you know anything about that he replied no sir, then he asked John. do you know anything about a tape from the Director of the FBI office."

He wouldn't say anything, Andrew got two CIA agent's to lead him into one of the office's, Wade got the tape out of the top right hand drawer and handed it to the President and Sandy. then they all went into the room, where the agent's were asking John what he knew about the tape, when he saw they were going to find out what was going on he started talking, "about four agent's getting him to monitor the tape's for them, but only if Wade was involved, in any extra circular activities, that Wade's name, was the key to what they wanted to know about what he was up to, that he had over heard, them talking about, Wade was into some crazy stuff, and if they could get into some of it before Wade stuck his nose into it, it could be their ticket out of this crappy place, the President look at the CIA Director, then said "lets help them out of this crappy place," Sandy said "we've already got two of the name's, on the list of name's, John gave us, those two are incarcerated, at the Hover Building."

Doc looked at Wade, pulled him from the group, and asked if that wasn't conspiring to do their own thing, with in the CIA, it sound's like something that need's to be addressed by the Justice Deptment.

Doc said "the other two are looking for their cohort's and they're in Gastonia, N. C.", Wade smiled then said "you know this for sure, yes there staying at a Comfort Suite's, posing as sell's men.

Wade stepped away from Larry, pulled the President, Sandy and the CIA Director, together told them what Larry said "about the other two being in Gastonia, N.C."

He came back, told Doc, "we need to get to that location, PDQ, he fliped his cell phone open, and called Gary at Stony Knob, when he answered, he told him "We needed to be there," Gary asked where are you, Wade told him to them up in the parking deck no. 1."

Wade indicated to Sandy, that they were going, they walked fast and were in the parking deck no.1 in twenty minutes. when they got there, Gary was standing halfway out of a concreat wall, waving for to them, Doc and Wade then stepped into the compound at Stony Knob.

Doc was looking around for Erin, but didn't see her, then he asked Gary where she was, Gary told him I think she is visiting with you Mom and Dad in Adamville.

He smiled to him self, and thought his Mom is checking her out, and that pleased him.

Wade told "Gary where he wanted to go, but first I need Russ he stayed at that the Hotel we need to go to," when he rounded him up, he put vest on them all with side arm's, Doc chuckled then said "Wade we won't need these thing's."

Wade smiled and said "I promised your Mother, I would keep you safe and That's what I'm going to do, these thing's are Insurance, if we need them we've got them.

CHAPTER 26

Russ put his hand on Gary's and they walked into the Comfort Suite's in Gastonia N.C., Russ brought them into a hallway on the first floor, Doc told Wade which room's they were in, Wade went to the desk, showed his badge, and got key card's for the door's, Doc lead them to the second floor to room number 208 Robert Doud, was staying, Wade used a snake site under the door, Larry was right he saw old Robert banging away on a young thing in his room.

He put the card into the door, and quietly sneeked into the room, Wade,

Doc and Russ were standing, by the bed before Robert knew they were there, Wade had handcuff's and shackle's on his leg's and tape acoss his mouth in minutes.

Russ and Doc looked at each other, Russ smiled then said "the man can do his job very well."

Doc helped the young woman, with her cloth's, then said "sorry for the interruption, she smiled, at him, then said "you could be next," if you like what you see.

Doc smiled then said "I like what I see, but it's not for me!"

Wade patted her on the butt, look at Doc, you are a wise young man, then he escorted her from the room, and told Russ to keep an eye on Mr. Doud that he and Doc had one more room to check on, they walked softly to room 210, ran the snake under the door, Wade saw Brook's Wild, laying on the bed, on his belly naked, sound a sleep, he turned to Doc and said "that young lady has been busy this morning."

He put the card into the lock and gently opened the door, he and Doc were beside the bed, Wade started to smack him on his ass, to wake him up, when Larry fired his wepon into the mans hand, and Brook's firearm went off into wall, Wade said damn, I didn't see the gun in his hand, he had him cuffed, shackled and tape over his mouth. he turned to Doc smiled then said "I saw his hand under the pillow, but didn't think he was awake, so thank's."

Doc got a towel for the bathroom, and looked at Brook's hand blood was flowing pretty fast, he took a belt from a hotel bathrobe, and it stopped the flow of blood, the bullet went between the bones in his hand so it was just a flesh wound, but he knew it hurt like hell.

They finally got cloths on them, and Brook's hand bandaged, by a paramedic who gave him a shot of pain medication, that would last for the rest of the day, Wade turned to Doc, smile and said "I've got a new nick name for you, Doc Hobart," Larry smiled then said "I kinda like it to, as I am a Doctor."

Russ was calling him "dead eye dick, for saving Wade's butt, he could easly forget that nick name."

But would keep the Doc. he knew Brook's was going to shoot Wade, so he was ready for it, and he could handle a firearm, his grandparent's Bob, and John and even his Dad could shoot accurately.

But he would not tell his Mom, he knew better, Wade had everthing ready to go back to the compound, at Stony Knob, they locked these two in the brig and were recording all their conversation's to see if there were any other's involved in this little travesty.

Doc. asked "Wade what would happen to them, he thought they should be prosecuted," Wade said "he thought it would depend on their service records with the company, it could be they would only get a slap on their hand's, but it could also put them in prison, or they could send them to far off place's, who knows, they just want be assigned back to where they are presently."

Doc. "sound's a little crazy to me."

Wade smiled and said "I know what you mean, but the power's that be will make those decisions."

Russ, asked Wade" if he thought they would let him, get back to a normal life after catching those culprits, that caused all this crap?"

Wade said "well Russ, you have a unique situation, an Island that has the fountain of youth, if it ever got out that it even existed, who's know what some people would do to have it."

Doc said "that's what happened at home, the old folk's got some of that water, the night before I came with Wade, they were banging the the wall's, and having a ball."

Russ told "Wade that he wanted life back, and now!" He replied, "well Russell, "lets wait a few day's and see what we can get out of the 2 agent's and if they're the only one's involved!

I think your in the clear, and we can go build our place in paradise."

Russell smiled, "now that sound's like a plain," Doc "where is this place," Larry smiled, "oh wait, he told Russ's where it was, gave him the latitude and longitude," Russ looked at Wade, "how did he know that, I've never told a sole." Larry said "sorry Russ, it's just one of my ability's to know things, sorry, I gather Wade didn't know about it ether!"

Russ said "Wade you better not tell anyone what you heard," Wade smiled, looked at Doc "I guess we have to include you in our plain's, what do you think Russ," Russ replied, "sure just don't tell anyone else, let's get Gary and see if he can take us there, if he can do that he's part of our plain, and part of our family."

When they got back to the door room, Gary told them that "Sandy wanted those two agent's in the Hover Building this after noon," Wade said "damn we just got them settled in brig a few minutes ago."

He looked at Doc and Russ, "would you fellow's help me get them back to the Hover Building, this after noon," Russ, Doc looked at each, other Russ, said "the things you have to do for your friend's," Wade "Ah, come on it wont take us, no more than thirty minute's."

Gary opened the door, into the secure area of the FBI building, there were four agent's waiting for them.

Wade said "that didn't take any more the ten minute's, are you guy's happy,"

Russ asked Gary to do him a favor, let Doc see if he can take us to the Island, I think he know's where its at, Gary smiled and said "only if you let me fill my tank up with the water."

Russ replied of coarse, Gary started preparing his hose's, and had them ready, when he opened the door.

Russ asked "Doc to put his hand on Gary's arm and go to the Island Larry smiled at Russ, and Gary opened the door to the Island.

As Russ stepped onto the Island, "crap, now that's three of us who know where this place is, Gary had his hose into the lake, and was pumping water to Stony Knob.

Doc was looking around, then said "this place is beautiful, I'm not sure you should develop it," Russ said "we are not going to bevelop it, were only going to build us a home, Wade and I have already got plain's to build it."

Doc asked "what are you going to do with the water, there's a lot of old people in this World, who could use it's services."

Russ said "I never considered, selling it, I'm not sure I could, it's really not mine, it's something I discovered."

Doc, "well you could become very rich, and you wouldn't be have to charge a fortune, for the public to buy it."

"It's a discovery that need's to be out there, can we duplicate in a lab, it sound's like you could get a Noble prize, for having discovered it."

Russ asked "Wade if the government lab, had reported it's finding's?" Wade looked at him, "you know I haven't heard a word."

"They've had enough time, to respond, so I guess we'll have to start asking why!"

Doc asked "if he could taste the fruit, that grow's on the Island?"

Russ, said "Wade, sense, he's a part of our faimly, we should give him the grand tour," he smiled, "let's do it!"

Russ lead them to the top of the rock with the water running out of it, when he went around and crawled into the cave, Wade told "Doc to follow him in," when he got inside he marveled at how beautiful it was, then he asked if

"they had carbon dated the rock yet."

Russ looked at Wade, "did anybody think about that?" Wade replied, I'm not sure did the President do it, when he got the cutting off the tree's?" Russ

"I'm not sure, but it wouldn't be a bad idea before we leave," just as he said that, Gary came into the cave, and asked "what are you doing giving Doc the grand tour."

Russ replied that's it, "they were done in 30 minutes, Doc as he ate the fruit tasted Martha's peach cobbler, something he always loved to eat. then they scooted back to Stony Knob, where Doc wanted to be, he was looking forward to spending some

time with Erin, when they all got back to the house, he asked
"Janice if she was here, she told him, I think she is still with you
Mom and Dad."

He smiled and said "I might have to go home," he looked at
Wade, "what do you think?" he replied, "well Doc I think you've
done all the President ask you to do, but do you see anything out
there that we should attend to, Doc said "crap, Wade there are
more people involved in this than the four we've got, I already
know some of the names, that should be rounded up!

So I guess, we should go back to Washington, but I think I
need a few days off from the everyday grind." Wade smiled and
said "there are more important things for a young man to be
thinking about."

"So lets take a couple days off, I'll talk to Sandy, and the
President to see how we want to proceed, with this, does that
sound good for you!"

Doc smiled and said "I think we are thinking of the same
thing's because Lola is on your mind!"

Wade chuckled and said "you young man, are very, very
smart, Gary came into the room, and said "Janice wants to know
if we are hungry," "I think, I could eat a bit what about you
guys?" Wade looked at Doc, I don't know about you, but if she
has some of that French apple pie I want some!"

CHAPTER 27

Russ, Wade, Doc, Gary Sr., Brent, Sabrina, Sherry, Gary Jr, and Janice were laying away the French apple pie, nobody was talking, just eating, Russ's cell phone rang, when he answered, "he exclaimed What!" he looked at Wade said "Bow and Bobby have three more lashed down at my house, there were four but Bow sent one to Gaston Memorial Hospital he put a slug in his right shoulder, that was bleeding bad, he said he thinks he will be alright, but to get our butts down here and pick them up, before he shoots them to."

Wade looked a Doc smiled and said "the best laid plains of mice and men."

Wade and Doc had wapons, but on the way up to the compound Gary stopped at the county office and got his gun for Russ, "I hope you don't need this but if you do, you'll have one to, Russ thanked him, and as they were walking into the compound, Russ said "boys I think were the three musketeers," Gary said "there's four squad's of Marine's inhouse today you think you might need any of them?"

Wade asked "Russ if he thought we needed any help? Russ said "Bow is an ex-cop so I think he has things in hand, but just in case, Gary don't shut the door until we find out just whats going on!"

When they steped into Russ's house, they all headed toward the kitchen

Russ stepped into the Kitchen, "are you guys eating my groceries again!"

Bobby said "no I bought these, we cleaned you out last time, we were here,"

Bow smiled then said "Russ you have to get away from these people they're going to get me killed," he hugged Russ

Bo looked at Wade "there's 3 in the same bed room, the other one in the Hospital, I asked some friends of mine at the Gastonia police Dept. to guard the dude at the Hospital, until the FBI can pick him up."

Just as Bo was talking to Wade a spray of bullets came through the windows in the back of the house, they all hit the floor, Wade immediately looked to see if Doc was Ok, then he told Gary "to get a squad of Marines quickly," he was back with them with in 3 minutes.

When they got there Wade told "them where the bullets came from and told the squad leader that they should go out the front door and circle around the house keeping in mind this is a neighbor hood." in a little while there was a fire fight, and things got quiet, then the Marines came in the back door carrying, the bodys of two men, the Squad leader told "Wade they gave us no other choice."

Wade told "them to get the three in the back bedroom, then he told Gary to take them back to Stony Knob, and put them in the brig, and call Sandy and tell him what happened, and I'll take care of these two, and Gary was gone, then he asked Bow if he could get two body bags for these guys.

Russ got four sheets to wrap them in so they wouldn't bleed all over Russ's tile.

Bo & Bobby left to get boby bags from the Gastonia morgue, Larry told Wade "these are the names he saw," he pulled out their wallets gave them to Wade, found a pen and paper, wrote all their names on it handed it to Wade, then said "the dead ones are Jack Morton, Frank Marsh

Sam Swarts is in the Hospital, Bob Moss, Joe Barns and Jim Knoks are the three Gary took back to Stony Knob."

"I'm sure we got them all, but I'm not sure the powers that be will think so, Wade, what do you think?"

Wade responded, "there were more CIA people watching me than I could possible believe, and I never knew it."

Russ smiled and said "I sure hope we got them all, I'm getting tired of this crap."

In about thirty minutes, Bo and Bobby came back, with the body bags, Wade helped them put the two dead men in them, Bobby ask Russ "who's paying for the mess those guy's made, the windows, there's glass every where!"

Russ asked Wade, "what he thought about getting the Fed.s to pay for all the mess," Wade smiled and said "good luck, getting the Fed.s to pay for anything these day's."

"The CIA will deny, that they had anything to do with any of this!" Larry "maybe the President should take a hard look at Mr. Ward, and see if he can tie any of this to him, ten people in his origination have broken the law, and they should pay for their crimes."

Wade said "I think your right, I will tell him theres something rotten in Denmark and its beginning to stink."

Larry told Wade "we should spend the night with my folks in Adamsville"

Wade smiled and said "sounds like a plain, to me," then he turned to Russ and said "I don't think you should stay here tonight, you want to go with us over to Adam's Manor?"

Bo spoke up and said "your staying with me Rusty Willow," Russ smiled told Wade "I need to spend some time with these two guys." Wade said "there packing heat, and you have Gary's gun," he said "Larry thinks we've cleaned up the threats, and I'm inclined to agree."

Wade asked "Bo if he thought we could store these to dudes, in the Gastonia Morgue with out complications," Bo said "sure we could mark them FBI hold until they could pick them up," Wade asked "could you get them picked up tonight," Bo replied "sure it might take thirty minutes or so, but I could get it done."

When the bodys were on there way to the Morgue, Wade and Larry were on their way to Adam's Mountain, and Russ and his buddy's, would spend the night together, Wade would pick Russ up tomorrow.

On the way to Adam's Manor, Marty was telling Larry, "he had missed him for the past few day, where have you been, I know I didn't take you any where," Wade told him, "He's been helping the FBI for the past few days,"

Marty sighed, and said "helping the FBI, Wow."

Just as he pulled to the front door, he said "Larry Hobart, you take care of youself, Larry told him, "thanks Marty, but I can take care of myself."

He and Wade walked into the house, Doc's mother was the first to see him, She told him, "why didn't you call, let me know you were coming?"

"Mom we were in Gastonia, rounding up some bad guys, and I thought we would come home for the night."

Jeff heard Mary talking to someone, came to check on who it was, when he saw his son, he grabbed him and was hugging him, Larry "Dad please your embarrassing me."

Jeff said young man, your Dad is going to hug you as long as he can, he kissed him on his cheek. Larry started laughting, and said "I know and I love you both," he pulled his Mother into the hug with them.

Then Jeff noticed Wade standing there, Jeff "so your the reason I was embarrassing my son," He shook Wades hand, turned to Mary, "remember Mr. Hound," sure, "how are you," "fine thank you, we had to come to Gastonia, and Doc wanted to spend the night at home, so here we are," Jeff said "I'm glad you did," Mary said "we have a guest that staying with us that might interest you."

Wade smiled then said "I think that's the reason your young man wanted to come home for the night, if her last name is Messer."

Mary smiled and said "how did you know she was here?"

Wade smiled we've been through the door, a few times sence we last met Janice Pepper told us "she was here for a visit."

Mary said "she is with the Moms and the Dads, they love her as much as we do."

They all walked into the den, when Erin saw Wade she got up and hugged him and then Larry, she smiled and said "fancy seeing you here, the last time I saw you we were at Stony Knob."

Larry. was embracing her, George came to life, and was poking at Gracy,

Erin smiled, at him, then whispered "I think your going to be embarrassed if we don't maneuver, our selfs out of here and quickly."

Larry smiled at her, then said "how are we going to do that?"

She said "I going to turn around, and you stay behind me, until we can figure out just how to do that!"

They were close to one of the leather chairs, and they both backed up to it and Larry sat down and Erin sat down on the arm of the chair.

Jeff punched Mary and whispered "did you see that?" she whispered, "yes love our son has grown up." then Mary said

"I think we should think about sleeping arrangments for Mr. Hound!"

She asked him "if he needed anything, shaving, tooth brush gear, Wade smiled then said "all of that, will be needed, I just assumed we would be back at Stony Knob for the night."

Until Doc wanted to spend the night here, Mary "Doc?" Wade smiled, said "yes Dr. Larry Hobart, I gave him a nick name, and that's what I've been calling him," I hope it doesn't bother you Mrs. Hobart she smiled and said "I'll just have to get use to it, he has two Doctorates

That we are really proud of, but being a Mom, he's still our little boy at least in our minds."

Bob and June, Lucille and John got up and told them that they were ready for bed, hugged Larry and Erin and told them to have a good night, as John walked away, he turned and winked at Larry.

As Bob walked by Wade he told "him he would show him to a bedroom, that would have every thing he needed, Mary said "thanks Dad!"

Then she turned to Jeff, "do you think we should chaperone these two, after all she is visiting us, and I think from what I saw going on between them, her parents might not like it to happen, in our home."

Jeff smiled then said "honey do you remember what you told you Mother the night we met, that you would show me where I was going to sleep!"

Mary smiled at him, then said "honey, you remember what a great night that was."

Jeff told "her go to bed," then he handed the key's to the cottage to Erin and said "If you two need some privacy, you could spend the night down there!"

Larry smiled at Erin, and shook his head yes, and she did the same.

Jeff hugged them both, then left them by themselves.

He knew he would let Jake find his Nellie, because he was remembering his first night with Mary and the joy there of.

Larry and Erin were so engrossed with each others bodys, then Larry told her about something his Father told him about his Mother, "that the first time he saw her, he knew he would be following her around for the rest of his life and that's the way I feel about you." she kissed him, and said "I know and that's the way I feel, and somehow you Mother told me I was carring around Gracy, she didn't actually tell me verbally, but the first time I met her I was aware of that name.

And I finally asked her about it, she told me the story about her faimly, and it went something like this, that the Graymore family women knew their vaginas had names, that it was something she knew from birth, and that it went back in time to before the cival war." she smiled at him and said "now ain't that a hoot," Larry kissed her and said "well love, George wants to get into Gracy as quickly as possible."

And they were down to the cottage in no time, and their night of bliss lasted until the sun came up.

Jeff called the cottage to see if they were up yet, when Larry answered the phone, cheerfully, "yes Dad we're up, and Dad we should get a Judge."

I've asked "Erin to marry me and she said yes, so we should do it as soon as possible."

Jeff said "well son I think we can get it done today, but first let me tell your Mother she will be pleased and happy to know, she wanted you to start a family for some time now, so as soon as you two get ready come on up to the house!

You know Martha will want to feed you two, as soon as possible, and you probably need the nourishment after last night, Doc chuckled then said "yes Dad I'm hungry and I'm sure Erin is to!" they showered, and up to the house, with in twenty minutes, when they walked into the dinning room, everyone eating at the table, stopped and "congratulated them on the decision, to get married."

Wade said "I guess that means you won't being going back with me to Stony Knob or to Washington?"

Doc smiled "I guess not, although we will have to talk to Erins folks, this might be a shock to her parents!

But we've decided that it will be." Wade smiled and said "Brent and Sabrina are pleasant people, and if that's what she wants I sure it will be OK with them, Erin said "my Mom and Dad will give us their blessing I'm sure" Jeff called the Messers, and "informed them that his son had asked Erin's hand in marriage, and she has excepted."

CHAPTER 28

Brent, Sabrina "how do you wish to proceed, they want to get married today," Brent said "today! Well Mr. Hobart, let me talk the rest of the family and I'll call you back!"

Brent hung up the phone, and smiled at Sabrina, and said "your daughter wants to get married today."

The Hobarts "want to know where the ceremony will take place, here or there?" "They would like it to take place at Adam's Manor, but will do what ever we wish."

Sabrina talked to her parents to get there thoughts, and they all thought it would be great, for Erin to get married, at Adam's Manor.

Sabrina called Mary and asked "what time, and what she should do, it's the parents of the Bride responsibly."

Mary told her "it would be a privilege, for her to take care of the wedding.

They want to ger Married on the big rock at the cottage, which Jeff and I are very pleased that they want to do it there. its always been our favorite place to hang out, and Jeff feels like its his home."

Sabrina asked are we limited on who could come, Mary said "well I would think just family and a few close friends, is that all right with you?"

Sabrina said "it would be!"

But my Mom and Dad, and of coarse my Brother and his wife, Wade and Russ are already there, so Lola, Betsy will come with us, that's ten people from our side."

Mary said "that's sounds good to me, my whole faimly will be there!"

Sabrina told her "we would have to come early, because of the door and the security for it!"

Mary told her "that Jeff had arranged for a judge to be here for the seremony the kids didn't want anything fancy, come casual, and come early as you want the wedding is at five." as Sabrina hung up the phone, she smiled at Brent, and said "our daughter is getting Married, today."

Brent said "that's just how it should be, love, starting another cycle of life

I wonder how many grandchildren we will have?"

Sabrina smiled at him, and said "if I know my daughter she will have already started down that road, with such a goodlooking young man as Larry Hobart."

She and Brent informed all of those who would be going to the wedding what time to be at the door, they would be leaving at three o'clock for the wedding at five o'clock.

When Gary and Janice got to the door, Betsy, Lola, Gary Jr., Sherry, Sabrina, and Brent were all there with smiling faces.

When they all stepped into the cottage, at Adam's Manor, Russ and Wade were there to greet them, and told them that the kids were up at the house, that if they wanted to go up and of coarse Erin Mom and Dad, Granny and Gramps all road up to see their baby.

Gary Jr. and Sherry, Russ and Betsy, Wade and Lola walked down to where the people in charge of the wedding, were setting up an harbor for the ceremony.

Gary Jr. was "telling them that this was his first visit to Adam's Manor and he thought it was one beautiful place."

The people setting up the arbor, told them "to get some of the covered chairs and have a seat at the edge of the big rock, that it was so peaceful that one could spend a life time just listening to the sound of the water running past."

When they all gathered at the edge of the big rock, looking down at the water, Russ said "I think we could get attached to the sound of the water as it flows past the rock," he was holding Betsy hand, he kissed her, and said "it reminds me of our water fall."

On our island, at least I hope its ours, she winked at him, and replied its ours because your the only one who knows where its at, he said "well love, I'm no longer the only one who knows where it is."

Betsy said "honey who else knows where its at?" Russ replied, Wade and Doc, Larry some how knows, he was telling me where it was, and in doing so Wade heard the location."

Betsy smiled at him and said "well love I don't think you have to worry about eather one of them."

Russ smiled at her, "if we had time we could strip and jump into the river, we haven't got to do that yet."

Betsy said "Mary told me we could do it sometime, but I don't think today will be that day."

Gary Jr. heard them talking about jumping in the river, naked and told Russ that sounds like fun to me to, Wade looked at Lola and said "we could do that to couldn't we, she smiled, you bet we could!" they all had been setting there for a good hour, when the wedding party came riding down the hill.

Doc and Erin seemed to be glowing, as they came down to where they were setting at the rock, and talked to them all, Jeff "hustled them back up to the cottage, and told them the Judge was up at the house, so if you wish to we could start a little early," Larry smiled at his Dad, "we are indeed ready."

Jeff told "Brent he would give the Bride a way, and I'll be best man, then Judge Trudy of television fame, walked up to Jeff and hugged him, and Mary then Bob, June, John and Lucille, when she got to Janice she said "pointing to Lucille that woman make the best ice cream in the world."

Janice said "doesn't she though," when she shook hands all around, she stood under the arbor, and here comes the bride music stated playing from somewhere all around, Larry and Jeff were standing wating for Erin to come to the arbor, Brent with a big smile escorted her, beside Larry, and Judge Trudy married them. they all went up to the cottage, Larry and Erin Hobart cut a cake, there were all kinds of pick up foods, that were delicious. and before anyone noticed they were gone, Sabrina asked "where they were Jeff told them, he had helped them get away, that they were on their honeymoon, that he had given Larry his personal plane to go anywhere they wanted to go, and they would be gone for a month."

"They will call while on there trip to keep us all informed, and I don't know where they were going, I think Erin was in charge of where they would go! don't worry, I have two top people watching over them, to see that no harm can come to them."

Judge Trudy, left and the people cleaned up the place, took the arbor and the sound systems away. they were all setting around talking, Betsy told Mary "she was going to get a towel and that she was going skinny dipping, when Russ heard that he looked at Jeff and asked if that was all right with him, Jeff smiled and said "sounds like a winner to me," he looked at Mary and said "you think we could to." Mary smiled, looked at Sabrina and Brent "would you like to to skinny dip, with us." Sabina looked at her Mother, who shook her head no! Mary looked at Wade, "are you going to?" he smiled looked at Lola, and she said "I'm in," Sherry looked at Gary Jr. and said no!"

When Bob, June, John and Lucille heard what they were talking about, John looked at the Pepper's, and asked "if they were going to jump in with the rest of the crowd?

Janice looked at Gary Sr. and said "we're not getting naked in front of all these people" Gary Sr. smiled at John I guess not!

Mary thought that her family would leave and go back up to the house, with the talk of going skinny dipping, but she wasn't sure about Papa John, but Lucille set him straight that she wasn't pulling her cloths off in front of all these people, and that he wasn't eather!

So Bob, June, John, Lucille, Gary Sr. and (Janice, Sabrina, Brent, Sherry and Gary Jr. headed for the Manor House.

Mary asked "everyone to leave their cloths in the cottage, and gave everyone two towels, that if anyone was modest that they could wrap themselves in one until they got into the water."

As they all headed for the rock, Russ was playing with Betsy bottom, his towel was pocking out in front, and it was obvious what he had on his mind when he got into the water. it set the theme, for the rest of the group, they were all hugging when they all got to the edge of the rock.

Jeff showed them all "where they could get out of the water, at the rivers edge and that he would put there towels down there so when they wanted to get out they would be there."

Jeff told "them if they wanted to they could walk down the steps to the water, that under the rock it was twenty feet deep, so you could jump or dive, its gets shallow around the edge.

Betsy did a beautiful swan dive and to see her beautiful naked body as soon as she came up Russ jumped into the water, Jeff picked Mary up and his towel fell off, so Mary was resting on his rather large woodie, he smiled at the rest, and said sorry!

Wade watched his beautiful wife Lola do a swan dive, the arch of her body the roundness of bottom, it turned him on, and when he jumped he was standing tall, with a smile on his face!

They were quiet for the first thirty minutes, because each couple were engaged in making love in the water, there were a few moans, and a few oh boys, but other than that it was quiet!

But after the loving, they were playful splashing each other, and having a ball just like children!

With warm body's in cool water, it wasn't long until they started drifting out of the water, Betsy and Russ were the first to get out of the water, she smiled as they walked up the steps out of the water, she turned and said isn't "fun, to be naked and unashamed in such a beautiful place like this!"

And all the men, were indeed admiring her beautiful naked body, but not a word was said!

Then they all got out, when they were all dressed, and setting on the deck at the cottage, eating the food left after the wedding. enjoying each other company, Janice, Gary Sr., Gary Jr., Cherry, Sabrina Brent, Bob, June, John and Lucille! came back down the hill, when John came up he said "no naked women here what a shame!"

Lucille looked at him, then said "you just better watch it old man" he smiled at her and said "just kidding love."

Gary Sr. told Wade that Andrew called him, looking for you, he said you didn't answer your cell phone, Wade smiled and said "I turned it off so no one could interrupt Lola and I, and Russ and Betsy, we needed a little down time."

Wade said "did he tell you what he wanted with me," Gary said "no but if I saw you, I was to tell you to call him that it was important."

Wade looked at Russ, it could be something about us building our dream Home on the Island, Russ smiled, then said "now that would be something I could get excited about, he looked a Betsy, wouldn't you love?"

She looked at him, then said "lets hope, that the other mess is behind us."

Wade said "well we will never know until we call Andrew, but I hope its good news."

Wade walked away from the others, pulled out his cell phone, found the Presidents number, and dialed it, after going through a couple of intermediaries, he finally got Andrew, the President told him that he had "fired the head of the CIA," and that they had all the bad guys except one deep operatives, and I'm talking about a nasty SOB, Delta force.

So its not over just yet, where are you now?" Wade told him that "Larry Hobart had just married, Gary's grand daughter, Erin, and had flown off to who knows where." that Russ, Betsy, Gary Sr, Janice, Gary Jr., Sherry, Sabrina, Brent, and

Lola and I, so sir how do you want to handle it."

Tell Gary Sr. to "open the door to get me, and let me talk to Mr. Hobart because, the way I understand it that those kind of operatives don't know when to quit, and that he's after you, Larry and Russ, that was his mission."

Wade closed his cell phone, then looked a the rest of them, he grimily said to Gary Sr. "Andrew wants you to get him here, as soon as possible," Gary looked at Jeffery, and asked him to come inside for a moment, Jeff replied "sure," when they got inside, he told him that "the President wanted to talk to him, and that your faimly shouldn't be here.

So if you would please somehow arrange it, he would be grateful, Jeff looked at him and said "my faimly should know about the door!

Gary Sr. said "no they shouldn't its all for their on safety," Jeff said sure then he went to the door, and asked Mary to come inside, when she stepped inside, she asked "what's up," Jeff told her the President wants to talk to us "could you somehow get the old folks back up the hill for a little while."

Mary got her Parents and her god parents, back up to the house, and came back the President was there with six of his Secret Service agents.

He told them to set down, "that he needed to talk to them, about Larry,

Russ and Wade, that his CIA Director, Harry Ward, and one of his Section Chiefs William Best started a covert operation, that nobody knew about for their on benefit."

He looked at Gary Sr. "Ward was the one that wanted your door, and when he found out about the fountain of youth!

He doubled his effort, when he found out that the FBI had all the men in locked up at the Hover Building, and the three dead men of his, sent Best over the edge of reason, and that's when he went for a deep cover operative his intention was to get rid of Wade, Russ and Larry."

"Now Ward and Best are faceing criminal charges, along with his men, but the agent he put into motion, will not stop until the job is done, I know that sounds crazy, but we live in a world that we need those kinds of people who will stop at nothing until he has completed his mission, we think we know the operative who is on the loose to get you three, Wade, Russ and Larry his name is Jack something, and we are trying to get a message to him that he should decease and desist this operation, but so far we haven't been able to contact him.

Usually when they go on a mission they disappear, they become what ever it takes to complet their task." then he looked a Jeff, and said "sorry for all this mess, but I would like to bring a company of Marines here to Adam's Manor until we can eliminate the threat of any harm to any of you." Jeff said "do you think we are in danger?" Andrew, said "yes we do!"

Andrew said "we could set the company up out side of your walls, with out any disruption to your lives."

But "we need to get Larry back here, he could tell us where he is, and if we could contact him, we might avoid any further problems."

"Then we could let Wade and Russ get on with their dreams, of a home on the Island."

Jeff said "I can get in touch with him, I've got a couple of strong arms with them to keep them safe."

He pulled out his cell phone, and got his son, and told "him about the President being here, and they have a problem, that would concern, you its about one other agent still looking for you, Wade and Russ."

Larry chuckled and said I know Dad, his name is Jack, Jeff said "son you talk to the President."

Jeff handed the phone to Andrew, he said before you say anything, "let me congratulate you on getting such a beautiful young lady as Erin," now we have a problem, Larry told "Andrew, that his Dad told him about it, our problem Jack is in Weaverville posing as a construction worker, is in room #12 of the Weaverville Inn, sir he's high strung, take it slow with him!"

Andrew chuckled and said "Larry you just saved us a lot of trouble, we were about to set into motion, a company of Marine's around you father's estate."

Larry said "I know sir, and tell Russ he has the his Island, I know it will make him happy."

Andrew said "yes son I will, and have a very happy honey moon."

Andrew handed Jeff his cell phone, and said "that boy of your's surprises me ever time I talk to him."

Jeff smiled and said "isn't he something."

The President then he told Wade "where Jack was and how Larry said to handle him that he was very good in his field."

Wade had the word out, to the Ashville FBI agents, "to just talk to Jack and tell him that the President has canceled his mission, and to report back to Washington for a debriefing on where his orders came from, and if he doesn't leave or agree, to take him out, discreetly, but be very careful, this guy is one of the best in his field." Andrew apologized to Jeff and Mary Hobart, and to the Peppers, then said, before I go, I need some of Lucille's best ice cream," Mary got him and the Secret Service men, a goodly portion.

Andrew didn't linger long, but he did finish his ice cream!

CHAPTER 29

The President left with his Secret Service escorts, Wade went back to Stony Knob, with all the Pepper's, when Wade got there he called "his friend Jack Short and laid out a plan to recover Jack Loot, or discharge him, he wasn't sure just how it would go, so he asked Jack to get five more FBI agents out of Charlotte over night so they could get Jack tomorrow by some form or fashion," he also got four Ashville Cops to watch his movements, he told them not to spook the guy, to not even approach him, just to watch his movements and keep him informed as to where he was and what he was doing.

The next morning, one of the Officers, called him and "informed him the man, had only went out for breakfast, and was still in the diner eating!"

Wade met with Jack and the other agents, just outside of Weaverville three of the Cops came to the meeting, and left one at the diner, watching their man.

Wade made sure they all were protected but in plain cloths, and went into town in three's, two were milling around in front and two were doing the same in the back, the rest walked into the diner, and ordered coffee, the Cop pointed Jack out, and they clustered close around where he was Wade walked up and sat down in the booth with him, and showed him his badge, and told him "what the President said, that we were to escort him to Washington."

For a debriefing, Jack responded, "he would indeed stop his quest, that he hadn't been able to penetrate the Stony Knob security, and wanted to know what was up there, that warranted having the Marines there."

Wade told him that "the President, has a compound there, which he often visits, with his friends the Peppers."

Wade asked, "then you are willing to go with me, back to Washington, and sort this mess out?"

Sure Jack said "the President is my boss, and I like him, he's a fair man."

When Wade "called his troops to gather," Jack chuckled and said "you came loaded for bear."

Wade smiled and said "We didn't know just how you would handle being told to stand down from a mission."

The more Wade talked to him, the more he liked the man, Jack told him "it was just a job, that he was good at, and they recruited me in Nam, for my shooting skills, that he was a damn good sniper.

And that he kinda like the life style."

Jack had at Jet lined up for the trip to Washington, Jack collected his gear and they were off to Washington, and the President sorted the mess out, and charged Ward, and Best with conspiracy.

When Wade and Jack got back to Ashville, Wade visited for a while with his old friend and his family.

But when he thought about Lola, he told them "he was now married, and needed to get back to her."

When he finally got back to Stony Knob, he stoped at the Pepper's house Russ was there with Betsy, Lola and the girls, he hugged his wife, and told Russ "the President had given him his blessing, on building his home on his Island.

That Willow Island was under the protection of the U. S. Government with its valuable commodity, (the fountain of youth) that you always use it wisely and for the betterment of mankind.

When Russ heard that, he smiled and said "We've been waiting for that for a long time!"

Then Russ asked Gary Sr. "if he would think about bottling the water, and testing it out on a few Nursing Homes, to see if it would make a deference in the lives of the old people living there."

Gary Sr. said "it would be a privilege," then said "let me talk to Jeff Hobart he might want to get in on this, Russ then said "Mr. Pepper I wasn't interested in making a lot of money on something as natural as what I've found on the Island, I just thought it was something I could do for other people."

Gary smiled and said "I wasn't thinking of a lot of money, in my pocket, but there would be a cost factor in such an undertaking, and I thought Jeff would help us with the startup cost of such a venture."

Russ smiled and said "I know with a business that it is essential to make a profit."

And so the Willow, Pepper and Hobart bottling company was formed, to dispense this wondrous product, they started in three nursing homes, with each patient taking one sixteen ounce bottle daily for a month, with a Dr. dispensing and monitoring the progress of the patients, with in a week each Doctor, showed a marked improvement, in each patient drinking the water and all the Doctors thought they had found a cure for old age, and with in a months time they felt sure it was a cure for old age.

It was such a success that the Federal Government started purchasing the entire production and distribution of the water.

With in six months, Russ, Wade, Bow, Bobby, Betsy, Lola, Susan, Gina, Gill Martha, Gail and Sheila had put to gather their dome home. they had three large generators, supplying the electricity. to refine the crude oil into deasel fuel, which ran all the generators.

Russ made sure that no containments, had been brought onto the Island that everything that had been brought here had been decontaminated, with all the latest technology.

The water was being transferred from the Island though Stony Knob with a bottling plant in Weaverville, and Adams Manor, with a bottling plant in Adamsville, everthing being handled with the latest sterile technologies to keep the water pure.

Bo married Susan, Bobby's wife had left him and took half of the two million, Russ had given him, and he was going to marry Gill. the remaining girls could sleep with whom ever they wanted to and often did, they were all just one large loving family.

Gina, Martha, Gail and Sheila, were as happy as anyone on he Island, and they were all proud of what they had accomplished together.

Russ had brought his plane back to the Island and built a first class hanger just where he first parked his plane when he brought it up the river below the lake, packed full of parts for it, but they rarely used it to go Island hopping. they used the door, because of the water being pumped form the lake

Russ wasn't looking for riches, but the water was in such high demand that the twenty five cents per bottle he was getting had already grown to quiet a tidy sum, in the millions.

He and Wade installed a hundred mile radar system, that talked to them if anything was approaching, a storm or any ships, or planes.

A satellite phone system that was clear as a bell, and received television signals better than if they were in the U. S., Bo, Bobby and their wives Gina, Martha, Gail and Sheila built homes close to the shore.

But most of the time they were at the dome home, because of the T. V. system Russ had installed, Bo and Bobby were in the process of cabling from Russ's system, to their places, Russ required that they put them under ground, they used a cable digger but it was still a lot work and that only came in spurts, sense they had worked so hard on building the dome.

Wade did still worked for the FBI, but only on cases he choose to do, but the President could still talk him into the ones he thought Wade should look into, but now Russ, Bow, Bobby and Larry. were working with him on all his cases

Wade had trained Russ and Bobby, Bow was already a seasoned Cop and knew a lot about Wade's work, but it was Larry. who knew about what was going on with all of Wade cases.

When they were all together Bobby call them the fearsome five and they were getting the cases Wade handled solved.

Doc and Erin had their first child, it was a boy, they named it John Wade Hobart, and for sure Papa John was pleased as punch, Wade was its godfather.

Brent and Sabrina nor the Peppers were getting to see the new baby as much as they would like, So the door was opened to Hobart inlaws, as Jeff thought it should be, so both familys were now going from each other homes, because of the Baby.

And back and forth to the island, so all three family's were becoming one large family.

Talked to each other daily, Jeff and Mary and Doc were taking care of there family's business's.

Doc and Erin were helping with the fountain of youth bottling business.

It was easing the suffering of a lot of old people who were now getting much younger, most of the nursing home business was gone, they turned them into condos for the people who had been living there as patients.

CHAPTER 30

Russ and Betsy were happy, living their life on the Island, they all had accomplished their dreams, and now were enjoying just living their life form day to day and it never got boring, they were all having sex anytime the urge hit them, which was three or more times daily. there were four men and eight lovely ladies, the old saying is make hay while the sun is shining.

And rarely did the sun not shine in paradise, so the job of the new arrivals on the Island witch was Bo and Bobby even with their new wives, fell on them to take up the slack, with the other ladies, and they preformed very well.

Bo had never been married, but manage, in his old life to snag a few lovely ladies here and there, in the process of his Police work, and was happy in his life.

Bobby had been married for a long time while running Russ's business and thought he was happy, Margie, was not demanding in their sex life, Bobby thought that was just the ways of a woman, he cared for her, but he was after the loving stuff in a woman, and never found it.

She never gave him a child, so he just poured himself into his work, she would complain to him, that he was never there, but when he made an effort for her she didn't change, her way toward him.

But when Russ his best friend, was gone for two years, and thought dead, that really messed him up, he and Bo and Russ had been together all their lives, they weren't brothers, but they had met early in life, just barly out of diapers, they all had lousy parents, and they bonded when they all three found a shelter under a big rock, in the woods, so when life got to much for them at home, they found themselves a home under the big rock so in there hearts they were brothers.

So when Russ heard that Bobby's wife had left him and took half of his money, and the President had turned them loose, he decided that his brothers would live and work with him and have a home on the Island and Wade thought he and Russ with his two buddy's could build their house on the Island.

When Bo and Bobby came to the Island with him, right away there were sparks between Bow and Susan, Bobby and Gill.

When Rusty's two friends came onto the Island, they were like a kid's in a candy store, because when they met all the beautiful women on the Island, their lives changed, they were making love to all the ladies who were not married.

Bow soon thought he had to have Susan, for a wife, and so they were married.

Bobby was still having troubles with his ex wife, but when he finally got a divorce from her.

He just had to have Gill, so they got married, but that left four unatached beautiful ladies.

Bo and Bobby were called on to help fulfill, the needs of the other four ladies.

And with all the girls being like sisters, it didn't bother them that Bo and Bobby were doing double duty.

Russ thought that sometime in the future, they would find mates, but for now Bo and Bobby were taking care of business just fine.

But on occasion, when the moon was full, Wade and Rusty had a go with them.

And for them all, life was very, very good.

On a Friday morning, in late December, Wade and Russ were down at the generators proforming maintenance, which thay had to do every three months, Bo and Bobby did it last, so it was their turn.

Lola called Wade, "told him the President had called and wanted him to call him back," he punched the numbers, and the President answered quickly, witch was unusual, Wade told him so, Andrew said "well we have some trouble that you and your team need to address."

And its cold here so dress warm, Wade chuckled and told "him that they were half naked and sometimes naked."

Andrew told "him that he would have warn cloths at Stony knob for them all and asked how long will it take you, to get ready?"

Wade "told him about thirty minutes," "I'll have Gary open the door in 3o minutes.

CHAPTER 31

Russ and Wade hurred back up to the dome, and told "Lola and Betsy that they would have to go to Stony Knob, that if they wanted to go with them they should get the other girls," Russ said "I think you will have to stay at Stony Knob babe, now you can stay here where it comfortable, or visit the rest of our friends there, the choice is yours. she kissed him and said I'm going with you love!"

He ask her to call "the girls house and find out what they wanted to do that he and Wade would get the boys," she called them but got no answer So he and Wade went to Bo house first, no one there, next to Bobbys they were side by side, went into the kitchen first and there were four naked ladies in the den, and Bo and Bobby were pumping away, Russ stoped Wade from interfering, when he heard them finishing up their chore, he slapped his hand to gather, they all jumped, and they both said "you bastard" they looked exhausted, Wade got some orange juice, and gave it to them both, told them we need to get moving, we are needed elsewhere.

It was a few minutes before they moved, then Betsy and Lola came in with Susan and Jill, their wives, and they were all laughing, about them getting caught with their pants off, when all of them finally got their cloths Martha, Gina, Gail and Sheila told the boys that they had done very good job Bo started laughing, we had just finished with our wives, and in came these four horney chicks, our wives told us we had to take care of them, they left, he looked at Bobby and smiled and said "I think we did a damn good job."

Wade told them about "the President calling and wanted them in the States that it was cold as a well diger butt, but he would have warm cloths for us so the question is do you ladies want to go with us as I said its cold, so its your choice, I would think that you will be staying at the Peppers or the Hobarts.

But we have to know fast, Gary is opening the door in thirty minutes, and its already been fifteen minutes.

Lola said "I'm going with you honey, all the other girls wanted to feel a little cool air and maybe some snow."

And that seemed to excite all the Ladies, when Gary opened the door they all stepped into the compound, he seamed to be surprised that they all had come, he told them "its cold out side and there is about six inches of snow on the ground. and I would like to go to the Island for the warmth, Russ told him "to go if he could," Wade "the President never told me what he wanted nor how long we would be away."

Gary said "I will let the kids have a couple of day apiece, and I know that will thrill them."

Russ told him "they had turned off all the electrical stuff not being used, but the generators were still be operating, so all they need to do is turn on the lights, the air is still running, all they need to do is enjoy themselves.

Gary "I'll will contact Jeff about getting more water, because I'm getting low at the bottling plant, I know sence we installed those hundred thousand gallon tanks, we thought we would stay ahead of the demand, but its running pretty close."

Russ said "sure, how are you doing now on getting it all over the U. S."

Gary smiled and said "well with the Government doing the distrubtion I think its already covering the entire country."

Wade walk up to them, told "Gary that the President wants us in Washington as soon as we can get there, that time was not on our side with the issue at hand."

Gary looked at him then said "must be serious!" Wade smiled then told "him, that it must be," but he didn't tell me what it was all about."

"But that he had the warm cloths here, to put them on that it was cold up here, there's was a foot of snow on the ground, the States were going to had more!"

Gary said "yes he told me to tell you to see Sargent Smith, that he would fix you all up with warm clothing."

Wade said "let me go see him," Andrew wants us there this after noon, so I guess its very important.

You know Andrew doesn't get excited about trivial stuff," Gary said "he was here for a week, last week, he and his wife, and there didn't seam to be any thing wrong, or he seamed relaxed to all of us."

Wade gathered Russ, Bow, Bobby and asked Gary "if Larry hadn't got here yet?"

Gary said "he's down at the house, saying good by to his family," he told "me he would be here in a few minutes, but he's already got his warm clothing from Sargent Smith."

Gary said "so you guys go get yours, and I'm sure he will be here by the time you get your's on."

Wade and his cohorts were off, to find Sragent Smith, when they came back they were in gray and white spotted military fatigues, that were made of the latest bullet proof material, their helmets were off white and side arms were off white to, when they got back to the door, Larry was waiting for them "he started kidding them about how sharp they all were."

Wade asked him if he knew what was going, with this assignment, Larry smiled and said "there are two Arabs butt holes, who brought into this country an Atomic bomb, they came through South America, one came in with the detonator, and the other has the bomb, but the good news is they are in two different States, one is Salina, Kansas, where the bomb is the other is in Kansas City, on the Missouri side, trying to get it together, but today theres about six feet of snow on the ground, and nothing is moving in the Midwest."

Wade said "I think the President wants us in Washington!"

Larry said "we should be going to Salina Kansas, and take care if the Bomb. before they can get the detnator mechanism to the bomb, and pretty damn quick, so you get the President here."

Wade called the President, and told him what Larry said about the bomb being in Kansas."

Wade turned to Gary and told him, "Andrew's in the oval office, open the door for him." he came into the compound, and grabed Lary hand and said "we only got the word this morning that there was a bomb in the country, and we didn't know where it was, so thank god you knew, where it is."

Larry chuckled and said "that's why you pay me the big bucks."

Andrew smile and said "you mean we pay you money, for crap like this?" then he said "if I remember correctly you wouldn't take any money from us Larry smiled and said "I know but you just couldn't afford my fees, for the crap I really do for you sir."

"Now what we need from you is the transportation, you know, the weather out there nothing is moving, and that's a good thing, in that Abdul is not able maneuver in weather like this either.

He's in a concrete block building just a mile and a half on 140 off I35 in Salina Kansas, he is armed with a handgun.

Now sir if you can line up a snow track vehicle that will hold all five of us, an experienced driver, Gary could get us close to where the vehicle is going to be, this will pass quickly, when we get the bomb, the problem will be solved.

The detonator for the bomb, is in Kansas City on the Missori side, Al Jabar is his name, he to is incapable of movement, he's in a Motel on fifty first St. just off of inter State 485.

If Gary can get us into an empty room there, we'll snatch him and the detonator and put them in a cell here until you can put them where they need to be.

Sir if you could get this done quickly, we could be on our way," Andrew looked Wade you need to add anything to this," "no sir I wouldn't, he put his hand on Larry's shoulder, what ever this young man says is good enough for me he's on a whole different plain, than we are."

Andrew looked at Gary and said "lets get the detonator first, that will give me time to get a snowmobile in place for them. then he looked a Russ, Bo, and Bobby "are we ready men? Bobby smiled and said "sir the fearsome five are ready to roll."

Andrew smiled "sounds good to me son," Gary get me back to Washington and you get them to Kansas City Mo.

Larry said "sir, that bomb could take out four States, and rendered them useless for at least a thousand years, so I suggest you find out from those bastards all you can to prevent this from happening again.

They put it in the center of the continental U. S. for maximum effect."

As the President stepped thuough the door, you bet we will do that son and was gone.

Gary said "we got you in room five its on the end of the Motel," Larry said "he's in room three, let me understand where he is in the room, before we move in on him," they all eased out of room five hugging the wall, and keeping low when they got to room three, Larry held up his hand, and

"whispered give me a second, then he turnd to the rest of them smiled and said "that A hole is on the commode and his gun is on the night stand toward this window," Wade pulled out a set of master keys, handed them to Larry eased one in the door, it opened, Bo and Russ moved to the other side of the door, Wade stood up in front of the door, asked "ready" they were in front of Al Jabar before he could respond.

Wade sent Bobby and Russ with the keys out to the truck, they returned with a case with the detonator.

Wade chaned old Al Jabar, his feet and hands, to make sure he couldn't escape, he walked to the motel office and told the guy at the desk not to call "the police about the truck, that a team of FBI agents would pick it up as soon as the weather permitted."

They took Al Jabar to room five, and Gary opened the door to the compound there were four Marines waiting for him, they put him in a cell's until someone could collect him, and stored the detonator until it could be picked up.

Gary told them that "they wouldn't need the snowmobile, the President had found a vacant warehouse next to the block building where Abdul was, they found a door they could get out of, and the snow was over their knees.

Larry told them to let him get close to the building so he could get a feel for what Abdul was up to, he stepped out side walked close to the building put his hands on it, and came back quickly.

He started stomping his feet to get the snow off his cloths, he looked at them smiled and said "this is our lucky day, Mr. Abdul is snoring like a salor sleeping off a drunk."

"Gary if you would lets go into his building," Gary shut the door and opened at the next building when he did, Russ and Bo went in first soundless. it was a large open space with a heater in the middle where Abdul was on a cot still snoring.

Wade slowly put the chains on his hand and feet, when that was done, they just stood staring at him, wondering if he was going to wake up, Wade walked over to a truck that was parked in side, he took out the keys and opened the back, he took out a rad meter, and checked to see if it was safe to move, he couldn't get a reading from it, so he thought it was safe, then he thought maybe he should call the president to see how he wanted to handle it. he fliped his phone open thinking that he might not get out with this weather but Andrew answered on the second ring.

Wade said "that was quick sir," he chuckled and said "I've been waiting anxiously to hear from you," "we've just got the last man in chains, I thought you might not want to leave this thing at the Peppers, sence they've given us so much over the years, and I personally don't want to take it there.

So where do we take it to, it going to take four good men to move it, unless we have a cart to roll it somewhere."

Andrew said "let me think about that for moment, then said, "who's in charge of the troops at Stony Knob?" Wade said "sir I don't know, I've been on the Island for most of the year, getting our home together, and its looking good, we love it there, and you should come see it."

Andrew said "I will I promise," but tell Gary the bomb is only going through Stony Knob, that I will instruct the Marines where to take it as soon as it get's there.

Can you guys get it into the compound, sure sir, when we get the other prisoner I want them in the FBI lock up in the Hover building and under guard.

When they steped into the compound at Stony Knob, Lt. Bask was there waiting for the prisoner, he sent him to the holding area, told Gary "that the bomb needed to be put in a safe place, Gary told "him to put his hand on his" and he opened the door, there were men in white lab coats who took the bomb into some place Gary didn't know, and when he shut the door he still didn't want to know where it was, and he would have a talk to his friend Andrew, that he didn't want this kind of traffic in his home.

Gary knew he would have to let Lt. bask back into the compound after takeing the two prisoners into the FBI lockup.

And he would end his day, Larry, Russ, Bow, Bobby and Wade went to the house.

CHAPTER 32

As they were leaving he heard them talking about some of Maria's French Apple pie, that was on his mind, he hoped they would save him some, then he thought of his wife (his sweet thing) wouldn't let them eat it all and not save him some.

Then Lt. Bask was back, he went to his quarters, Gary got into a cart and road down to the house, went strait to the kitchen, they were all setting around the table eating French Apple pie.

And talking about their day in the field, Larry was telling them just "how nasty the bomb was, and what it would have done," Wade said "I thought it would really mess Kansas up, but he didn't realize it would get four States."

Russ smiled and said "we should get medals for saving this country.

From wreck and ruin, that if four middle States were uninhabitable for that amount of time, who knows what would happen, to this country.

Larry looked at him, then said "probable every third world country would pounce on us, and who knows what would happen, to our way of life."

So fellas we were lucky today, Wade spoke up, and said "I don't belive any third world country could take us down."

But that's just my opinion, Bo said "I'm with you Wade, we may have to open a can of woop ass, but we could still do it.

Erin walked in with the baby, Larry just had to kiss her and hold his son, he was one proud father. he asked if his parents had called today? Erin smiled, and said "honey you know they did and wanted to come up here, but the door was tied up with what ever you guys were doing today."

Wade said "we were never in danger, but we saved four States from being bombed out of existence for quite a few years."

Erin said "I don't think I needed to know that!"

Gary walked in and said "there had better be some French Apple Pie for me Janice said "honey you know, I saved you a whole pie for you," Bobby said "what and I only got two pieces," she winked at Bobby, and said hes the one I sleep with and winked, Bobby smiled and said "Oh "I know what you mean."

Then Russ asked are we going back to the Island tonight, or are we staying up at the compound, Gary said "your staying with us, I've got two children on the Island for at least two days. I promised them that, Mr. Willow and Mr. Hound, so you have to stay at least one more night."

Bo asked the girls if they had fun playing in the snow, Jance said "they were like a bunch of children making snowmen and throwing snow balls at each other.

I was with them half the time, and we had a ball, didn't we girls," they all said "yes."

When Gary had down his third piece of pie, Janice put a stoped to him eating any more.

When they left the kitchen, they moved to the game room and started playing pool, some were playing cards.

Gary was the pool shark, and was taking on all comers, and one by one he set them all down.

Until Betsy started playing strip poker, and Janice put a stop to her pulling off something, she politely told her that she didn't want Gary seeing any of their beautiful body parts, Larry and Erin had already left the house to be together.

Betsy smiled and said "we had better go up to the compound, and finish this little game, and they all told the Pepper good night."

They all road back up to the compound, then went into the day room, but there were eight Marines, setting around watching television, as soon as they walked in, Betsy looked at the rest of of the party, "we can't play in hear the President would have a fit if we played strip poker in here, we would corrupt these nice young men, whom I'm sure are horny as hell,"

Martha, Gail and Sheila, looked at each other, when Russ saw the look on their faces, he knew he couldn't let that happen, he knew there would be hell to pay if did happen, so he personally escorted all four ladies out of the day room, told them that he just couldn't let it happen in this place that if they all played strip poker, he was sure that there would be enough woodie's around to take care of them all."

And indeed after they were all striped naked, there was indeed enough to wood for all eight ladies.

They were up late, and in the morning they were all slow to get moving, when they decided to take showers, the men went in first, but were slow to get bathed, So Betsy lead the ladies into the shower, but as soon as the men saw all the beautiful naked bodies, it was off to the races again and it was two hours before they all got dressed.

When they went to the mess hall they were serving lunch.

And after lunch all the girls wanted to go shopping in Asheville, then they wondered if the roads were clear, so they all headed down to the house, to find out if they could go shopping, they all went in the backdoor Janice and Gary were drinking coffee.

Gary could tell the ladies were, excited as they asked "if they could go into Asheville shopping?

Janice said "I think the roads have been cleared, and looking over at Weaverville, the traffic seams to be moving ok."

CHAPTER 33

Gary smiled at his wife, and she saw him, then she said "ladies we could go shopping where ever you wish, how about N. Y., London, Paris and even Las Vegas?" Betsy said "wow you know that would be a place I would love to go to, she looked at the other girls, what do you think?"

They were all shaking their heads, yes, Janice said "Caesar's Palace has a large shopping mall in it.

And I bet the Guys would love to play the slots, while were shopping so I know one fellow that would love to do it, she looked at Gary and winked he smiled, said "I'm going with you babe, you know we've not beem there for quiet a while."

So they rounded up all the guy's, Wade, Russ, Bo, Bobby, Russ told them that we need to take Larry, so he can pick out the machines we play, he should be able to pick some winner's for us.

So wade called the appartment they were staying at beside his Erin answered the phone, Wade told "her about them going to

Las Vegas for the day, that all the ladies wanted to go shopping at Caesar's Palace, did she want to go?"

She said hang on a minute, then asked "Larry if he wanted to go to Vegas she replied yes, But "we will have to take the Baby to Adam's Mannor, we'll be right over or should we meet you at the compound."

Wade said "we'll pick you up, as we go up there ourselves."

When they all got to the compound, Russ ask "does anyone know what the temperature is in Vegas?"

Larry "told them it was in the low eighties. but the casinos were cool in the seventies, so what we have on should be OK, you might have to unbutton your fatigue shirts, but the people in the casino will wonder about our garb and when we fleece them, of some of their money, they'll be watching us closely!"

Gary opened the door to Adam's Mannor, Bob, June, John and Lucille were the only ones at home except the staff, Larry told them what they were going to do, June tooked little John right away, Larry asked where his parents were? Bob told him they were at the bank, taking care of some business, Russ said "to Bow and Bobby we could get some money form our boxes and wouldn't have to use Mr. Pepper money."

Gary had loaned them a thousand dollars a piece, Larry spoke up and said "you want need any more money and you can pay Papaw back out of your winnings.

Or do I have to give you play by play description, on whats going to happen when we get there."

Wade said "no I don't want to know until it happens," Russ me eather, Bo and Bobby agreed."

Larry said "let me call them, I don't think my Mom and Dad has ever been to Vegas before."

When Jeff and Mary got back home, Gary opened the door, "told them to wait until he could check to see that they didn't walk into a crowd of people out of a wall, that would take some explaining and we don't want that to happen."

When they all stepped out there were eleven women, and seven men, Larry told them to stay to gather at all times, then when you ladies get through shopping you call me and we will put the package just inside the door and you can come to the casino to."

They separated and the men walked out onto the casano floor, Larry told them to let him get the feel for the floor, and the floor was pack, but the high dollar slots were mostly empty, as he moved and was touching the machines when he found one that would pay he set them down at it and told them to bet maxmun bets after he got them all set down it wasn't long until the jackpots were pouring out and the casino personal were watching them like hawks.

Larry was having a ball, watching them, until a man came over and asked what kind of uniforms they were wearing, he motioned Wade over to talk to him, Wade pulled him aside and showed him his FBI badge, were testing a new theory on how to supply money for the Government. through the casinos of America.

Wade laughed out loud, then said "we are only here for this evening, we are working off a little steam, having a ball busting your butts, and we are doing a pretty good job of it, do you have a problem with that." the guy smile and said no not yet? But we might just have to run you off in a little while!

Wade set him down very abruptly, and told "him that he had just threatened an Agent of the FBI.

And he had better get his ass out of his face, before he decided to put him under the jail," the guy scooted as fast as he could.

Larry came over and patted him on the back, and said "way to go boss."

Wade smiled at him and said "I'm not the boss young man, most of things we've done together you've solved all the problems for us before we even get started."

Just then Russ hit a jackpot that set off the bell and whistles the pot was twenty five thousand.

And the group crowded around him, when he was finally paid off, he gave Gary five thousand dollars to cover their loan from him, Larry lead them out on to the floor looking for a really big progressive jack pot, he felt of the machings, smiled and said "lets get some serious money from these guys." the jackpot was twenty five million dollars, and with in thirty minutes the Bells and whistles, really went off Wade had won twenty five million dollars that would be paid out a million a year.

The girls came up to them with their arms full of packages, and were congratulating "him for his good fortune," and they wanted Gary to go with them to get rid of their burden of packages.

When they got back they were all anxious to play Erin kissed Larry and said "honey pot, show me a good machine, and he did, she sat down for ten to fifteen minutes, and hit a jackpot of ten thousand dollars, all the other girls required the same service, and they to hit jackpots. they played until one o'clock in the morning, until the casino started acting funny, and Wade started noticing how they were acting, he was about to lower the boom on them then looked at his watch and saw what time it was and knew they should leave.

He gathered them all to gather and told "them we should get out of here that it was really late or early," Jeff said we should, he didn't have room in his pocks for any more money, the rest had money stuffed every where, all the ladies bags were filled to the brim, they had given Wade a milliom in a satchel.

And as they passed the eight big guys watching them, Jeff stoped at each one of them and gave them five hundred apiece. when Wade saw this he opened his bag and gave them a banded stack of a thousand dollars, and that brought smiles to the faces.

They walked quietly to where the door was, there was no one around to disturb their exit form the casino.

When Gary opened the door it was to the Hobarts home Jeff, Mary, Larry and Erin stoped there they got their packages, and as they started to leave Jeff empied his pockets of money into the shopping bags of all the ladies they all protested, but Jeff smiled and said "it just a token of the fun you gave us today, good night, we love you all."

Then Gary opened the door to Stony Knob, they stoped at the desk by the door, Russ wanted to know how much money they all had gleaned form the casino, as best they could count in a short notice, they figured they had a little over three million, that was counting Wade million, Russ laughed and said "we had better not show our faces in that casino ever again, we're probably on their do do list."

As Gary and Janice started down to the house, Wade and Lola were walking with them, Wade asked Russ if he wanted to go with them to the appartment next door sence Larry and Erin stayed at the Hobart's."

He looked at Betsy smiled and said "do you need us to be alone for the night," she smiled, then said "not after last night love!"

They all showered, but no sexual activity occurred, in the shower, they all seamed to be to tired.

Russ put on some clean shorts and climbed into bed and closed his eyes he thought he would be asleep in no time, but when Betsy climbed into bed she was naked as a jaybird, he felt her get into bed, he automatically pulled her into his spoon position, and soon realized she was naked, he started automatically playing with her breast, and with her bottom next his crotch his body quickly started responding to the feel of her butt, he slid out of his shorts, the sweet smell of her body and the love he felt for her, he had a full erection, she chuckled, and said "I thought we were tired," he said "I guess it has a mind of his own," he positioned her bottom for rear entry, entered started pumping with vigor, it wasn't long until his joy erupted, then he fell fast asleep.

Until five o'clock in the morning, Betsy woke him up, and required his services, he quickly responded, when they finished, fell fast asleep, until ten o'clock in the morning.

Bobby was knocking on their door, when they woke up, he was fussing at them to get up, they both rushed to get showers and dressed, everyone else had already eaten, but the cook in the messhall had saved them food, when they finally got there, they were hungry.

CHAPTER 34

As they were eating Wade walked in sat down and smiled at Russ and said "we are going to get medals for our work on the A bomb deal."

The President will here be in a hour and a half, and he wants all of us there I think all the Hobart's will be there, the Peppers, I think that Gary's getting a medal to for all his efforts for us.

Lola said "doesn't that sound exciting, it dose to me."

Betsy put her arms around Russ and said "it dose to me to!"

Russ said "you really don't do things to get madals for doing them, its just part of ones character."

Wade smiled and said "that's true, but I think that when one is recognized for doing something that's worthy of being recognized is very special you can't deny that?"

Russ said "I guess I can't argue with that!" Betsy smiled and said "Teachers are often looking for accolades in their work, but hardly ever finding them, but I guess just seeing, the kids, grasping and understanding what they are being taught, is reward enough, what do you think Lola?" your right honey, to

see a child, struggling with their studies, and if you can find that
spark in them, that opens their minds, to the possibility's, that
education can give them, is truly a joy to any teacher.

Bo, Susan, Bobby and Jill walked into the messhall, Bo asked
Russ what what going on?

That one of the Marines told them that "they were to be in a
meeting with President, in twenty minutes."

Wade looked at his watch, then said "I guess we should go, we
wouldn't want to keep the President of the United States waiting
would we?" they all got up and walked out of the messhall, Russ
asked "Wade to lead the way that he didn't know there was a
conference in the building.

Wade said "yes there is I think the Marines us for meetings,
that he had only been in it once."

When they got there, two Marines were standing guard out
side the doors when Russ and the others walked into the room,
there was a room full of people, then he saw it was all the Hobart
clan and the Peppers.

The President was standing at a lectern, he smiled at Russ as
they all set down in the front row, Larry and Erin were already
seting there.

The President said "good evening to you all, I'm glad you
could come, I would like to began with an explanation, what I'm
about to do will not be on the news or any publication.

What all five of you did in Kansas will not be publicized in
any form or fashion, except for a letter that will be put in the
archives that will be marked secret and will never be brought

to lite, because it would scare the bejesus out of the nation, if it were know that an A—bomb was placed in the center of the Unite States, the ramification, if it had happen, would have been disastrous to this country."

Now having said that, it gives me great pleasure to be able to present to you the Presidental medal of freedom, as I call your name please step forward to receive it.

CHAPTER 35

Wade Hound, when he gave him his medal and shook his hand, he said "this man has been working for our country for a very long time and deserves every accolade this country can give, and a very good friend"

Next—Larry (Doc) Hobart when he gave him his medal he said "this young man is the smartest person I've ever met, and the brains behind this whole operation, and I consider him a good friend.

Next—Bobby Rice, Bo Arrow and Russell Willow, will you all three come up here please, these three guys have know each other sence early childhood and although there not brother in birth, they are in sprit, as he handed each a Presidental medal of freedom.

Bob is an astute business man, Bo has been in law enforcement with a very fine reputation in that field.

Capt. Russell Willow, Russ looked at him funny, he had totally forgotten his Military career, he had wanted to put it behind him, because of the loss of all his friends.

The President looked at him, "I see you are surprised, that I know all about your career, I am sorry to say that if our friend Larry hadn't brought it to my attention.

I might never have know, or looked at your records, but I am proud to give you, your just rewards now! I belive you are one of the most decorated. Pilots of the Koren war.

But never received any of them, I talked to your flight commander, he told me that losing all of your comrads in arms, all seven of them.

That you wanted to get as far away from the military as you could, but the most important medal, was when you were shot down, in North Korea, you brought seven good men back to safety, that all seven of them, wanted you to receive it, and pushed that you should have it, and I as Commander and chief will see that you get it.

The Medal of Honor, he asked Wade to get the case, to show Russ what all was in it."

The Medal of Honor, the Distinguished service cross, the Distinguished Service Medal, the Silver Star, the Legion of Merit, the Distinguished Flying Cross, a Purple Heart and the Presidential Medal of Freedom.

Then he said "Russ I've know Generals that only had a few of these, and it is an Honor and a Privilage to be your friend."

Russ with tear runing down his cheeks, Andrew said your going to have to say a few words to the good people.

He dried his eyes, smiled and said "(wow)" that's a lot to throw at fellow, what can I say, "as I look out at all of you, I know I'm with a group of very good friends."

"And the more I walk down this road of life, that is all that matters is having good friends like you."

"Boy" the Medal of Honor, "I'm not sure I deserve it, I didn't do anything, that given the same circumstance's, anyone of you would have done the same thing," then he smiled, "when I met those guy's in the jungle they were indeed lost, and I showed them how to survive, and with my navigational skills showed them the way back, when we were back in South

Korea and found our units, we were all banged up, they all thanked me, and I thought that was good enough.

I didn't think about it any more, but now that I think of it, I lost seven good friends, and saved seven good friends.

So there's the peace my mind I sought for a long time, about losing all of them.

Mr. President, I thank you, and Larry for reminding me that it was only that I needed more education, that lead me down that path.

The only sad part I never used any of my G.I. schooling, I just figured out that money was more important, than knowledge.

And with Bobby watching the bottom line, we became successful, in our business.

Bo, was already in law enforcement but after we were marooned, on Willow's Island, and got back, I twisted his arm and he came to work for us.

I thank you all for being patient, with me, I think of my self as a damn good pilot, and have had one hell of good life, and I have some of the best friends a fellow could ever have. my wife is looking at me to close my little speech out, but she is another reason I so very lucky, Thanks."

When he stepped down from the stage, every one came up looking at all his medals. the President told every one he had to leave, but let me do this before I leave "he stood at attention, and saluted Russ, and said every person in in the military must do this for you son, gave him a hug and left.

When Gary came back he had his medal hanging around his neck, with Gary, Sherry, Brent and Sabrina looking all tan and relaxed. they thanked Russ for letting them enjoy a couple of day in Paradise.

Russ said "you don't have thank me, your all family, and can come any time you wish," you can even build a cottage on the island if you want to he looked at Jeff and told "him, you can to, we are all faimly, I think you know that"!

Gary came over and he and Jeff did at smart salute to Russ, Jeff said "you know we were both in the Army.

Russ smile and said "I knew you guys were," Wade walked over and told Russ, "I think we should go home, this cold weather is nice for the Eskimo's, they can have these's temperatures."

But give me those nice balmy breezes of Willow Island, Gary said "you better watch out we might all move in on you, right Jeff, hey he said, that sounds like a good idea, what do you say Russ?

Well you guys can build any where you like, we have the dome, which can house all twelve, of us, Bo, Bobby and four of the girls have built cottages closer to the coast, but they did that for more privacy, if you know what I mean.

Jeff smiled and said "I know what you mean, I have problems like that around Adam Manor."

Russ said "the dome, is well equipped, we have air conditioning for the whole dome, eight bathrooms with showers, there are bedrooms all around the rim of the dome, that can sleep at least twenty five people, and from these rooms you can see all around the Island, the front section is one large den, with two large T.V. screens on each side, the reason for that is some times to keep piece in the family, because sometimes some people want to watch something else, if you get my drift," Gary chuckled and said "I know what you mean."

Russ continued telling them about the dome, you feel as if you were out side all the time, and the stars at night when you cut off the lights, is simply magical, oh, and the moon when its full, I think we all start howling, and the fun begans, now we sometimes go around naked, not feeling any shame, so be prepared if you come live with us, I guess we could get some togas to wear if our nakedness were to bother anyone, he laughed and said "especially if the President were to show up, with the first Lady.

Jeff smiled and said "yes that would be interesting," but I would think after awhile you would start using less clothing to, right!

Gary said "before the water, I didn't want anyone to see me in the buff, but now I feel comfortable in the nude, and things are well in my bedroom, and don't tell the Misses I said "that, she might put a few bumps on my head."

Russ and Jeff both laughed at that, Janice walked over and wanted to know whats so funny, then she looked at Gary, just what did you say old man, he smiled and said, "honey Jeff just told us a joke, I'll tell you later, sweet cakes."

That seamed to satisfy, Janice's curiosity, she walked away, Gary said "wow that was close."

Russ began telling them about the state of the art satellite system, for TV and phone service, we also have a hundred mile radar system and visual at fifty miles that's something Andrew had installed.

I think its for his protection, when he visits here, it will also warn us of storms coming our way, we are literally a country unto ourselves, but the President asked us to fly the American flag, and we are all good Americans

Jeff asked "how much did this set you back, price wise," Russ smiled and said "well lets just say half of the money you bought my company for is now gone."

But how much does a fellow need, we have every thing we'll ever need, and the water money is growing rapidly, I don't know how much we have in that account, I let Betsy administer that, she giving it to charities, I want her to be sure its not wasted, on originations that feed on people who will give, for their on selfish needs or wants.

And there a hell of a lot out there that's doing just that.

Wade said "and we built on top of an extinct volcano, we don't think it will erupt anytime soon, we hope!"

Andrew had the rock samples he took from the Island, tested and whoever tested them told him they were over four billion years old, and that's almost the beginning of time."

Jeff (wow) "that a very long time ago, it just might be the fountain of youth that history has passed down through the years."

Betsy walked over took Russ's arm, and said "honey lets go home and get native again, he smiled and said "that sounds like a winner to me love.

Russ told Bo, Bobby to get everone ready to go home, they seemed happy to do that, Jeff said "I want to go look at your home, if you don't mind,"

Russ smiled and said "sure and if you would you can stay for a while and go native with us."

Jeff said "that dose sound tempting, let me talk to Mary and see if she interested," we have so many irons in the fire, and I to don't need anymore money.

When they all got to the door, Jeff told Bob, June, John and Lucille that "Russ had invited them to look over, there new home on the Island did they want to go and look, it over?

June said "we had better got back to the Manor, but sometime we would like to see it, if that alright with you Russell, he smiled and said "you can come anytime you want Mom.

She hugged his neck, thanks Russell I will, Gary opened the door to Adams Manor, and they were gone.

Gary opened the door to the Island he, Janice, Wade, Lola, Betsy, Russ, Bobby, Jill, Bo, Susan, Jeff, Mary, Gina, Martha, Gail and Sheila all stepped into the dome, when they first walked in Betsy told Russ not to turn on the lights, just the night lites, when Jeff, Mary, Gary and Janice first saw the moon, shining so brightly threw the dome, Mary said "WOW that's the most beautiful site I've ever seen, Jeff smiled and put his arms around her, and said "gives you goose bumps doesn't it love."

Thay all sat down on the couches, and were just staring up at the moon and there was some hugging and kissing for a good ten minutes, until Bobby started howling like a dog, and that started everone laughing, Russ looked at Jeff, I told you we did that sometimes.

Jeff said "I can see why one would do that, its so beautiful, then he let out a howl himself."

Mary put her hand over his mouth, Jeff smiled and said "let out a lyric of you and me together uh hum."

And that brought another round of laughter, Russ said I think we should turn on the lights.

And show these good people what we have here, Gary spoke up and said "this is good enough for me."

Russ had a romote control in his hand, turned on the lights, there was no glair just a pleasant glow of light, you could still see the moon out side but muted a good bit, Russ asked Bo and Bobby if they were staying the night or going to their places, they looked at their spouses and the other ladies

Gail smiled and said "I think we should go home," Bobby smiled at Russ then said "we'll see you tomorrow OK." Russ said "good night".

And they were off, Russ told Wade to take over he had to the little boys room, Gary and Jeff said "we need to go to, then the all the ladies spoke up and said we right behind them.

When they had all assembled, back in the den, Jeff asked how they handled the waste water?

CHAPTER 36

Wade told "him that they recycled every thing, that it was our idea to do it, there are three large tanks, on the back side of the Island, that collect it, Russ and I didn't want us to pollute the Island, so when it goes through them it is pure again, and is flushed out to the sea."

Russ said "that's the reason we try to keep any out side contaminates off the Island, and so far we're batting a thousand."

Gary said "that what we do at Stony Knob, we recycle all the waste water until its pure, and then we use it on the lawns, but I have a service that keeps my systems working."

Russ replied we took courses from the company we bought the system from And even the girls can work on it, if they have to, Jeff said "sounds like you've got all the bases covered, on every system you have."

Wade smiled, "we think we do, and so far any one of us can fix what ever problems we have."

Gary spoke up and said "Jeffery lets spend the night, I want to take advantage of that beautiful moon."

Jeff looked at Mary, she smiled then said "I in the mood for love, lover she giggled at that."

Jeff looked a Russ then said "I think if you will have us, you'll have guest tonight."

Russ put his hands on both Gary and Jeff's sholders and said "I've already told you, your family, and family's come's first, right Wade!

"You got it Rusty", Russ said "ladies let Betsy show you the bed rooms so you can pick the one you want."

Gary smiled and said "hot diggedy dog."

Jeff laughed at that, and said "if you can't get a little strange, get (it) in a strange place."

Wade smiled, "that doesn't sound like you, Jeff," I know, I was just reacting what Gary said, "but I do think this will be a night to remember."

Russ said "before you go to bed, let me show you our TV system, he picked up the romote, and a large flat thin TV droped from somewhere above, we get all the latest movies, we've tapped into some ones movie channels,

Wade thinks that it's the Saudis."

And I could care less where it comes form, as long as we're not having to pay for it, but I suspect as long as we been receiving it, they can't tell we're getting it."

"Here let me show you what else they have piped in, he changed channels and there as big as life some bude was banging away on some beauty, the ladies wont want let us watch if there around."

Betsy brought the ladies, back into the den, she said "Russell Willow you turn that mess off right now, Russ replied yes Mother."

And cut the system off, he said "honey I was just showing, how good our TV system works."

Gary said "turn the lights off and let me look at the moon again."

Russ said "OK but not for long, when you go to bed, you will see it's just as clear, as in here, and I think it will be much more satisfying laying next to the one you love!"

Gary chuckled and said "honey are you ready to go to bed," Janice smiled And said "if you are ready, I am to honey pot," and they all smiles on on there faces when she said that.

Then she said "follow me love, I know where we're going to sleep," and they both said "good night to everyone."

Jeff looked at Mary, we ready love, she smile and said "you better belive it honey." and they were gone.

Wade looked at Lola and said "come on honey pot, its been a few days" and they were gone.

By the time every one left, Russ was standing there looking at Betsy, with a nice Woody, she looked at it, and said "lets go honey pot I'm horny to and they went to there bedroom.

When Gary got to the bedroom, he was ready, they never turned on a light the moon was so bright, like a large ball of cheese, they just shuked their cloths, and were in bed, he pulled her to him, and said "lets just look at that moon for a little while and we'll build a memory of this night." but it only lasted a few seconds, and he couldn't wait any longer and they were at it, twice during the night, Gary finally went to sleep stairing at that big ole moon, humming the hallelujah chorus, until Janice finally slaped on his arm, but he just drifted off to sleep.

Jeff and Mary, that is Jake and Nellie, were at it as soon as they climed naked into bed, after the first round, they lay on their backs looking up at that beautiful moon, thinking of their son, Mary said "lets build Larry a dome home down by the river, I think he and Erin would love it, sure we could do it, but I would like to keep it a secret, do you think we could pull it off," let me talk to Russ and Wade and find how they did it.

I think they had it all moulded in Japan and shipped to the Island and they put it all together, and they did a hell of a job, because its beautifully done if we could get the ground work done, and the plastic ordered, and have everything ready, it might not take to long to put it together, remember I got you cottage built in a weeks time, and I don't think it needs to be as large as this one.

Jeff giggled and said "Jake is standing up again, Mary felt of it, and said well Nellie sure is willing, and they were sexually active again, when finished and were cuddling each other, Jeff went to sleep, while Mary was still gazing, at what she thought was a magic moon, she lifted her hand to tough it, and went to sleep.

Russ and Wade had been gone for a few days, and they were horny buggers Russ turned Betsy every way he could, until they were satisfied, and they to fell asleep, Lola turned Wade everyway she could, until she wore him out and they to went to sleep.

When the sun came up and woke them all up, and every one had visited bath room's and had showered, they were all ready for the day, the old saying bright eyed and bushy tail, they all drifted toward the smell of coffee, they found Russ drinking coffee, and eating a slice of eggplant, the sun was still low in the horizon, but was almost as beautiful as the moon last night. they were all setting around a bar, on the side of the den, drinking coffee eating eggplant, uncooked, and each one was eating something different or what ever each wanted, it to taste like, Wade said "this stuff is the damnedest thing, I see it clearly, but I am tasting link sausages, and eggs with toast with orange marmalade.

Jeff and Mary were eating some of Martha's flap jacks, Betsy asked "Russ if the President was able to get this to grow in his wife's greenhouse?"

"No he couldn't get it to root, and grow, but he did tell me that it never rotted or went to the bad."

Which "I find very strange, don't you?"

Janice said "not any more strange than Merlin's door, she and Gary were having the same thing as Wade!"

Gary said "if you think about it, the water or the fountain of youth along with this purple eggplant looking fruit or what every it is?"

Janice said "and us with Merlin's door, Jeff and Mary with a son who knows everything.

Lola smiled and said "sounds like a bunch of flakes," Betsy said "oh no not at all it sounds so magical to me."

Think about it we have a food supply that gives us what ever we want to eat and its growing on this Island, then gives us the fountain of youth, it just has to be magic."

Mary said "she's right, why else are we all together," I want to know if you all had as much fun last night as we did."

Russ smiled, and said "looking at the rest of them, this was you first time on the Island with a full moon, we've experienced it often, and sometimes your mind and body works automatically, as I think you all felt it last night.

Lola said "the urge to make love is the most magical thing in life and on this Island its very, very special."

Jeff looked at his watch, and said "how can this be, I got a signal from Colorado's atomic clock."

Wade pointed at the satellite, the President wanted us to be on eastern standard time, so when he needed to contact us, we would be on the same time schedule.

Jeff said "Mary and I were talking last night about a dome home for Larry and Erin, I need to know how and where you got the acrylic molded at?"

Russ pointed to Wade, "he's is the architect, who drew up the plains for this one," Jeff said "would you draw one up for my boy," Wade responded with our boy, you may have given him life, but I to feel like he his is my son to, it would be honor, to do it for them, I'll get started to day, I think I would have been an architect, had I not walked into the FBI office looking for a friend, and Mr. Hover saw me talking to him and said sign him up and I've been with them for a very long time."

Jeff said "we want it to be a surprise, so if you could get me the plains for it I think I could sneek the foundation in for it, listen to me that boy will already know what we're doing now!"

Russ chuckled, well a surprise it can't be, in a few minutes, Doc and Erin walked into the den of the dome, the first thing he said was sorry dad, I wanted my lady to see what you were cooking up for us, I already knew just how beautiful this place is, but I don't think she would know, until she sees it."

Erin and Larry went around the room hugging, each one of them, Mary asked where is Johnny, Grand Maw Messer wouldn't let us bring him, she was complaining she didn't get to squeeze him enough."

When Larry told me about how much fun you guys were having on the Island with a full moon, I told him we need to come to, then he told me about Dad going to build us a dome home down by the river," he said "you need to see the one on the Island."

So here we are, and I knew Uncle Wade and Uncle Russ would let me stay the night.

Uncle Gary told me to "tell Nana and Papaw that things with the, door were slow, to stay as long as Uncle Russ will let you!

Larry motioned for Gary to come over, he pulled out of his pocket a disk and handed it to him, it will play continuosly, until someone stop it, Gary looked, at him and asked is it what I think it is?

Larry smiled and said "it is, I looped it to play Glen Millers moon light serenade for as long no one stops it."

I could see the advantage, of playing it while the moon looks like a big ball of cheese, laying with the one you love.

Gary hugged him and said "you are a gem son," and we love you!

Then he asked Russ if he had a sound system, Russ replied the best we could buy, he asked what have you got, My gem of a Grandson brought a recording of Glen Millers moon light serenade, we needed it last night, would you play a little bit of it, Russ said "sure and put it into his system," when it started playing everyone in the room, stopped and was listening to the magic sound coming from the speakers.

Bo and Bobby came in and stopped, Bobby smiled and said "boy we needed that last night the moon was so fantastic."

Janice said "that give me goose bumps," she whispered into Gary's ear he smiled, then asked "Russ if they could stay another night?"

Russ smiled, then said "you know you don't have to ask, anytime you want to stay you can!"

Wade stopped the music, I know we needed Glen's moon light serenade last night but listen to this and started Glen's, a string of pearls, Jeff chuckled and said "they just don't produce sounds like that anymore, I like misic, some rock and roll, but Glen Miller was in a league all his own."

They all set down on the couches, and were just listening, to the sound of one of the most famous band leaders of his time!

Mary whispered into Jeff ear, one more night, love, Jeff smiled and said you got it honey, I'm sure they won't mind, he got up and pulled Mary in front of him, started dancing to the music of Glen Miller Band.

In a second they were all dancing with them, Russ played the string of pearls three times before they stoped dancing.

Erin said "when she sat down, I didn't know I was coming to a party."

Wade said "this is the first time we've danced in our home, and it felt really good."

CHAPTER 37

Betsy walked over and asked Erin and Larry "if they were ready for the tour, if your going to have a home similar to this you need to see all the finer points of our beautiful home.

She said "looking at Larry, I think I heard your dad say a smaller dome than this one, but with a large family, as you have, you might need one this size or larger?

Or else where am I going to sleep when I come to visit with you?

Larry smiled, "your probably right with all the Pepper's and Hobart's, the Willow's, Hound's, Rice's, Arrow's and the other four lovely ladies oh and the President, "you know he want always be in the White House and I hope we can persuade him to come this way and be with us."

Betsy smiled, "I see what you mean, we are truly a large family.

As they were finishing the tour, Erin said "I think I would really like this down on the river, what do you think love, Larry smile, "you know love where ever you and Gracie are is my home."

When they returned back to the den area, Larry told his father, "that he should build one just like this for the crowd we have," Mary said "you know, I think Larry is right."

Jeff responded he's right, that way Wade doesn't have to draw up new plans, we could just build it across the river.

What do you think about that son, Dad that's what I had in mind for us Wade could just order the acrylic panels.

All of sudden a loud noise came through the speakers, uga-uga-uga warning a vessal has crossed the one hundred mile radar limits of Willow Island, warning, warning.

The TV droped down showing a blip in the hundred mile range of the redar

Russ cut the warning voices off, looked at Larry, what have we got out there

Larry said "it's a Russian vessal, but the occupants, are Arabs, and the ship is fully loaded with armaments.

"I think we should call the President, to see if there are any air craft carriers close to our location."

Larry said "I know you have some stuff installed on the island, if push comes to shove."

We can hold our own, right fellows, Russ said "I don't want anything destroyed on this Island."

Gary said "we could get a company of Marines here PDQ if we need to should I do that now."

Wade was on the phone talking to the President, getting his imput, when he hung up the phone, "Andrew said there was no air craft carries, close to us but there were two atom class subs

within a twenty minutes radius of our location that will check
the ship out, and sink if necessary."

All the ladies were standing and looking nervous, until Russ
told them "if they wanted to, they could go to Stony knob." but
none of them were ready to do that, just yet, Russ smiled who
wants to go see what happens out at sea, Betsy said "no your not
you knucklehead I'm not ready to lose you just yet."

Russ smiled and said "honey you want, I know there's a
full moon tonight and if I thought I couldn't get back to you I
wouldn't go.

But remember I'm an ace pilot, and the plane I'm flying is
almost as sweet as you, love.

So Gentleman, who's game to go see the fireworks if there
is any, Wade said "you don't supose the sub's would fire on our
plane, do you?"

Russ "we want get that close, we'll fly high enough to get a
good view of what going in the water."

Bo looked at Bobby and said "I'm in how about you brother,
Russ smiled and said "I knew I could count on guy's."

Larry looked at his Father, lets go Dad, Jeff looked at Mary
and then at Erin then at Gary.

He said "Gary you should stay, and if need be, take the ladies
to Stony Knob but this is an adventure I don't want to miss, right
son."

With a minimum of argument form the ladies, Wade, Russ,
Larry, Jeff, Bo and Bobby headed for the hanger, that Russ's Plane
was in.

When Russ and Larry unlashed the plane, and got every one on board and backed out of the hanger, he headed down to the lagoon, Larry was the co—Pilot when they intered the Lagoon Larry said "Russ let me take her up,

Russ smiled sure son let her rip.

When Larry had her up and out of the Lagoon, Russ prased "him, for doing it so well.

I guess growing up around planes, you learned how, Larry smiled and said yes but my Mom, wouldn't let me fly until I went to school and got qualified on all the planes Dad has, I been a licensed Pilot sense I was thirteen, Russ looked at Jeff, he smiled "I told you he is the smartest kid on the block."

Russ gave "Larry the coordinates of where the ship was when they left the dome." twenty five minutes later, Russ told "the guys to start looking for the ship on the left side of the plane."

When Bobby sang "out got it!"

Then they all saw it, when they first saw it a submarine was on top of the ocean being shot at with some kind of missiles.

Wade said "that's not good, then he asked Russ you got any bombs on this plane?"

Russ chuckled then said "sorry Wade, I don't even have a rock to throw at them."

From above it appeared that the sub was diving, when it was under the water, two torpedoes came from the second sub one to the back side and one went to the front, and the Sub that submerged sent one to the center when they hit their targets, the ship exploded, with such force pieces were flying in all direction, Russ said "they must have had a lot of munitions on that ship."

Larry "they came loaded for bear, they watched from above as the ship sank quickly into its grave below.

Russ flew several times around where the ship sank into the water, but saw no survivors.

Then he said "that's a little like combat fellows, but only a little, when you in the thick of things in combat, you have to trust your instincts and know the capabilities of your aircraft."

Jeff said "it was a little less dramatic, than I thought it would be, but we saw it happen."

Wade said "I would still like to know what they were up to coming our way was it on purpose or did they get caught in the wrong place at the wrong time?"

Bo said "they shouldn't have fired on a US submarine, that's reason enough to open a can whoop ass."

Bobby laughed at that, then said "your right brother."

Larry said "they were after the water, and I think it was Ward, who sent them, but he's in prison."

As they headed back to Willow Island, their moods were changing to the finer thing in life, when they landed in the Lagoon and taxied up to Russ's hanger, they all help put his plane up.

The Moon was low on the harizon, as they all went into the dome, they were laughting and talking about the adventure of flying out to see the strange ship that had shown up on there radar screen, and how fast the navy had dispatched it.

When they got in all the ladies were full of questions, Russ sat them all down, then looked at the men and asked who wants to tell the story, Wade said "it was all you show capt. Willow, you tell it!"

Then he told them what they did, when he was through telling them, there were a lot of questions asked, Russ said "first I wasn't the pilot Larry did most of the flying, I only took control when we got to the ship, and you know what happened there.

Wade called "the President and told him what happened. and he told Wade he would let him know if there was any damage to the sub."

Some one turned on the Glen Miller music, and that lifted the mood of them all, and it truly turned into a party, when the moon got a little higher in the sky, someone turned off the lights and the room was flooded with

Moon light, and they started playing Glen Miller's Moon Light Serenade and the room got a little quieter, and that went on for about half an hour, and the dancers slowly started disappearing and all the mens pants were pointing toward the bedrooms.

During the night most of the men were keeping cadence with the music of Glen Miller.

When they were all asleep around three o'clock in the morning, the music of Glen Miller was still playing, when the sun came up. when Russ woke up and looked at his watch, he said "holy Moly it's nine thirty," then he looked at his beautiful Betsypo, and he made love with her one more time. when she looked at his watch, "honey we have guest," they took a shower together. Russ went to the kitchen, there was no one else there, he cranked up the coffee.

Then they came straggling in, wanting some of that golden brew, it was observed by Russell Willow that these people had a very good night!

When Betsy, Lola, Gail, Gill, Martha, Shela, Susan, and Gail all came in and sat down, he pored them all a cup then raised it to them.

"to our fifth anniversary on this beautiful rock, our home!

THE END